The King
OF
Dragons

The King

OF

Dragons

CAROL FENNER

SCHOLASTIC INC.

New York Toronto London Auckland Sydney
Mexico City New Delhi Hong Kong

ALSO BY CAROL FENNER

Yolonda's Genius

A Newbery Honor Book

An ALA Notable Children's Book

ISBN 0-439-14607-0

12 11 10 9 8 7 6 5 4 3 2   9/9 0 1 2 3 4/0

Printed in the U.S.A.   40

First Scholastic printing, October 1999

The text of this book was set in New Baskerville.

I wish to thank:

David Mix for his powerful novel about Viet Nam, *A Glimmer of Good-byes*, unpublished at this date, which supplied me with a true and terrible feel for that war

My writers' group: Bonnie Alkema, Ardyce Czuchna-Curl, Betty Horvath, Ellen Howard, Terri Martin, and Wendy Risk, midwives all, for assistance in the birthing of this book

My sister, Faith King; my mother, Esther Gerstenfeld; my brother, Andrew Fenner; and my good friend, Ann Worth, for insightful comments on the early manuscript

My stalwart husband, Jay Williams, for help with the dedication and for his understanding when my obsession with this story took so much of my focus

Architect Randy Case for technical information and for unearthing old floor plans, and Sue Case for cheerfully joining the search

Jean Worth Concannon for inspiring me with fascinating symbols of her travel into womanhood

The Willard Public Library for letting me plug in when an early snowstorm took away our power

And always, the graceful Margaret McElderry, my remarkable editor, who, after pointing out the difficult terrain I must travel, trusted me with the basket of eggs

Carol Fenner

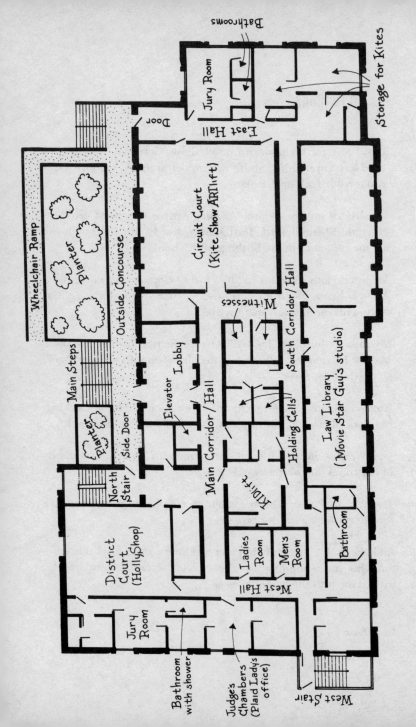

First Floor

Bathrooms

Jury Room

Door

East Hall

Storage for Kites

Wheelchair Ramp

Planter

Outside Concourse

Circuit Court
(Kite Show ART lift)

Main Steps

Witnesses

Planter

Side Door

Elevator Lobby

South Corridor / Hall

Main Corridor / Hall

Holding Cells

North Stair

KIDlift

Law Library
(Movie Star Guy's studio)

District Court
(HollyShop)

Ladies Room

Men's Room

Bathroom

Jury Room

West Hall

Bathroom with shower

Judge's Chambers
(Plaid Lady's office)

West Stair

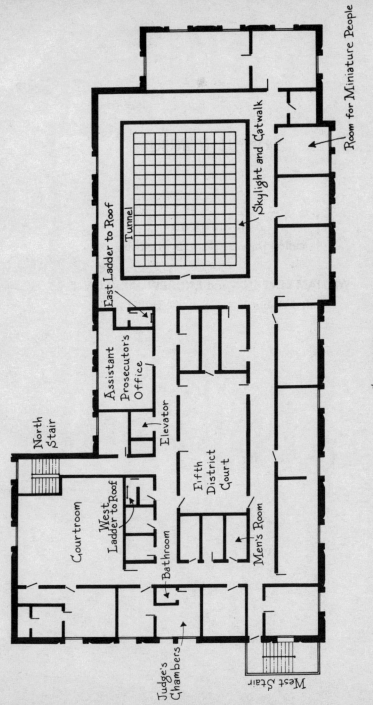

Room for Miniature People

Skylight and Catwalk

Tunnel

East Ladder to Roof

Assistant Prosecutor's Office

North Stair

Elevator

Courtroom

West Ladder to Roof

Fifth District Court

Men's Room

Bathroom

Judge's Chambers

West Stair

Second Floor

to the Fenner brothers

JOHN DAVID
called Dave the Rave by the twins

WILLIAM LEVERN II and **ANDREW JACKSON III**
called Dubby   called Andy

CHAPTER ONE

Intruders

The sounds below were what woke him. He had bedded down early, before dark, and slept lightly because of the hunger—probably only an hour or two. It must still be evening.

He knew immediately which room he was in. Sometimes, when he awakened, he was confused; sometimes he thought he was back in the small, neat room at the Squirrel's Nest Motel. Sometimes he shook himself out of bed in his room at his grandmother's farmhouse. This was truly odd because he hadn't slept there since he was eight. Two years ago? Three? He had forgotten birthdays.

Except for a faint glow from the hallway outside, the room was dark. Had he imagined the sounds? He held himself still, scarcely breathing. There were the noises again. It wasn't the sound of the weekly inspector, who flushed all the toilets on the first and second floors in the vast, old building and then took a smoke in the lobby, nor was it the noisy warnings of the occasional police sweep—doors opening and slamming, terse voices.

These sounds bore a resolute hum, even cheerful—women's voices, a man or maybe two. They were people who knew each other in a comfortable way. Not a family, not that kind of comfortable—children scrambling about, a father holding pizza in a box, a mother's voice like a net hauling the children in. A mother's voice. What would that be like, having a mother call you? If his mother had lived past his birth, would her voice have pulled him home?

Now he lay alert on his back, stretched out on the floor as he usually slept, listening for a while to the faint murmuring below until he was sure they were not moving about. They had not come to search; they would not flush the toilets. They would stay where they were.

The hunger he had gone to sleep with nudged him. Still he lay there and listened—listened for movement in the darkness around him, for the breathing close by that would tell him his father had returned, knowing as he did that he was alone.

Of all the rooms in this great old courthouse, this was the one he liked the best when his father was gone. It didn't have the two doors that his father always insisted on. *A room with only one door is a cage, Ian.* During the war, his father had once been someplace where he wasn't allowed out. But Ian favored this room over all the rooms in the big abandoned building. It had little arched windows at the floor level that only came up to his waist when he stood, as if this room had been made for miniature people. He liked the feeling of this room around him when he settled down to sleep, and he often lay next to the little windows and looked at the buildings across the way or gazed down into the street. He felt safe in this room for miniature people. His father felt safe in a room with more than one door.

Now the voices below quickened like music. He crouched, then made his way on hands and knees to the doorway, and looked out into the dim light made by the exit sign at the end of the hallway before he stood. Was his father trapped outside right now, waiting for these intruders to leave before he let himself in?

In the hallway, the voices could not be heard, and he stepped back into the room to be sure he had not imagined them. There were definitely sounds below, and they seemed to give off warmth. He wanted to get closer; he needed to reconnoiter (his father's word)—needed to reconnoiter the group below, find out what they were doing here. How much danger were they?

Ian could walk noiselessly. He had been taught by his father to move as though he were part of space itself. Slowly, not disturbing the air, he moved like a cat along the hallway. There were no creaks in the floors of the Hall of Justice, although the historic marker outside said it had been built around a hundred years ago.

He paused where another hall intersected the south corridor. Listened. The voices below seemed to come from what had once been a vast circuit courtroom. The judge's high platform (the bench, his father called it) and the witness stand were made of oak, his father said, as were the spectator benches. They were all in good condition, although the building, according to his father, had been abandoned for a number of years.

There was only one way he could get close enough to hear and not be seen. The ceiling over the circuit courtroom rose past the second floor nearly to the roof. It was made of frosted glass panels. Above the panels was the actual roof, and from this were suspended eight gigantic lights with great shades that directed the light through the glass panels to the courtroom below.

Ian and his father had discovered the space that housed the lights on a late September afternoon when reconnoitering the roof for entrances and exits. They had just moved to the Hall of Justice from an old railroad station that was being converted into a fancy restaurant. This roof had two entries from the second floor, one near Michigan Avenue and one near State Street. Ian's father always found the entrances and exits for every new place.

To get closer to the voices, Ian would first have to go farther away. To the roof.

One of the sky doors to the roof was in a little alcove next to a room marked ASSISTANT PROSECUTOR. He could not hear the voices at all in this alcove. He climbed the ladder that hugged the wall and gave the hatchway door above several silent nudges with no success. His father had always gone first and lifted up the heavy door. Now, ignoring caution, Ian gave a great grunting push and the door swung upward with a squeak and a rattle; one more quick heave and it locked open. Had they paused far below to listen?

The outside air was fresh and cold. It was already dark now, but he knew his way among the deep shadows cast from streetlights below. With stealthy crunches, he crossed the deep gravel on the roof to where a hut-shaped rise sat like a little building on top of a giant one—a little cabin on a moon of gravel. The door to it swung open easily.

He stood quietly in the doorway for a moment, savoring the voices that were now quite clear.

He stepped inside, closing the heavy door with great care, and paused on a little platform of steel grating. Listened.

A woman's laugh bubbled up from the courtroom below, followed by an answering chorus of laughter.

He crept down steel steps to a walkway that cleaved the long space into two equal parts, four great lamps on one side, four on the other. Somebody, a workman perhaps, had left a Coke bottle there on the steel grating of the walkway, an old-fashioned glass one, abandoned years ago, Ian guessed.

He crouched on the walkway, stared down into one of the frosted glass panels, which gave off a cloudy glow. He strained to see but the glass was opaque. Distinct as the voices now were, he could see nothing.

"Have you considered the amount of work?" A man's voice. It was one of those questions Ian remembered from third grade that don't require an answer. "Did you hear what I just said?" meant "I know you weren't listening."

"A lot of work for just six weeks," the man continued. "These benches have to come up. Where will you put them, ladies? You gonna take out the judge's bench, the jury box?" Ian strained his ears. Take out the benches?

There was a pause below. Then a woman's voice, low and pleasant. "Oh, you won't have to worry about that, Jerry." She laughed and, crouching against the metal grating of the walkway, Ian recognized the laugh he had heard earlier, only this time it was gentle and controlled.

"*We'll* get that done. What we want *you* to worry about is what help WGTV can give us in promoting the whole project. Can you give us free airtime besides the advertising we buy? We also need help hanging the show. Can you—can any of you folks—lend a hand in getting the kite show up? The museum will need lots of muscle."

Ian recognized that the woman was using her questions the same way the man had. But she was better at it; she flattered the man when she asked. Something about a museum. Ian thought about museums, full of old things—dinosaur bones or dark paintings. But kites? She had said *kites.*

"If you can do those two things, Jerry, we'll worry about the benches. We'll worry about what to do with the judge's bench and the jury box." Then they were coming here—for some sort of project.

Ian lowered himself to his stomach and lay there, arms tight against his body. Were he and his dad going to have company? Would these people come up to the second floor? Would Ian and his father have to leave?

Heat from the lights rose upward around him and the voices lifted upward around him. Momentarily his mind let go of the worry about his father. It was warm and kind in his spot on the narrow walkway.

"Here, Jan made these." Another man's voice. Ian was not lonely anymore, but his hunger came back. Below they were passing—what? cookies? and, his nose seemed to tell him, apple juice or cider with cinnamon or nutmeg—some comforting spice his grandmother had used in apple pie. Perhaps his hunger had made him invent the smell. He did what he had learned to do with hunger, ran his tongue over his dry mouth. He imagined eating. He bit into a cookie; he lifted warm cider to his lips. He chewed. He swallowed. Then he took a forkful from an imaginary slice of apple pie.

Below, the Lady Leader laughed again. They all laughed, it seemed. Ian had missed a part of the conversation during his play-eating. Now he made himself concentrate on the voices again.

"I'll need some help with publicity," said one of the women through the merriment. "We don't have much time to get folks revved up."

"First things first," said someone else.

Their voices wove back and forth beneath him, sounds mingled with spices and cookies and comfort. Ian drifted and dozed; the warmth from the lamps softened his bones. His arms relaxed and one of them slid over the edge of the walkway before he yanked himself awake. He lurched up in a chill of panic just as the great lamps went out. It took a moment for the exit light to feather the instant dark with a dim glow. Ian held his breath. There was a cold quiet below him. Far away he heard a door slam.

How long had the voices been gone? He felt the emptiness of the great building below. But he waited until he was sure no one had come back for a forgotten glove or notebook before he made his way from the roof.

The Hall of Justice was one of the best places his father had ever found for them to live. The old railroad station had not been heated and time had melted day into night. The Hall of Justice was kept at fifty-five degrees and its many clocks still worked. "They don't want the place to deteriorate, historic monument like this," his father had said. "Our luck, boy."

There were toilets here, too. All over the place. And soap still in the dispensers and paper towels. One judge's chambers had a shower in the bathroom.

9

"We can't use too much," Ian's dad had said. "Leave no traces." So they were sparing with the soap and even dried out the paper towels for the next day.

"Use a different toilet each time," his father had said. "That way the rust won't disappear from flushing. We want to keep it looking as abandoned as everyone thinks it is." Occasionally they took a careful shower.

In the beginning with his father it had been fun. Ian didn't have to get up for school. It was the best kind of adventure because it was real, not play; there was excitement in hiding for real, in finding a place to live, in surviving. Maybe the cavemen felt like this, Ian used to think. He had admired his father, who seemed so self-sufficient and clever. The hardest things had been not talking to people and being hungry a lot.

"Man can survive on very little," his father had told him. But Ian missed French fries, homemade cookies, and breakfast in a warm kitchen. He missed his grandmother's blue sugar bowl. He missed chatting with people, feeling the warmth of their interest. He still admired his father, but Ian's life was no longer the adventure it had been when he was only eight. Often he found himself envying kids going to school, walking dogs, yelling to one another. Being hungry was no fun. Not having a blanket was no fun.

They spent a lot of time in the public library, especially in winter. It was warm there. Ian's father liked to read and he stayed for hours among the history books or in the how-to section, letting Ian visit the large children's library upstairs. His father had instructed Ian to tell people he was home-schooled. That's why he wasn't in a regular school. They often used up the whole day at the library, reading, using the computer and the bathroom. Ian worried that the librarian would notice him enjoying baby books with lots of pictures. Once, during the first winter that he had been with his father, he had asked a young librarian for books for a nine-year-old. He wanted to know what kids in the fourth grade were reading. He had been a good reader in third grade. To his relief, the books weren't much harder. Words he didn't know he wrote down with a library pencil and looked them up. He enjoyed using the dictionary; it was what he thought real home-schooling would be like. Often he made up spelling tests for himself, wishing for a red pencil to mark 100% at the top of the library scrap paper. He couldn't take books out, but he had no comfortable place to take them to anyway. Even the Hall of Justice didn't invite reading.

Down in the old circuit courtroom, the smell of cinnamon and apples hung in the air; his nose had not been wrong. Ian discovered the intruders had forgotten to take the cookies! They sat, loosely covered with plastic wrap, in the center of a long bench in the third row. His mouth running saliva, he eased out two. *Leave no traces.* Then he took another one, careful not to disturb the plastic covering. There were a lot left, and he was certain the three wouldn't be noticed. He could even take four.

The four cookies made him hungrier, but he forced himself to walk away. He crept along the main hallway, crouching to pass by the windows of the wide entrance doors, then paused in front of the elevator. His father would most likely come through one of the side doors less visible in the block-long building, or he might use the hidden door by the north stairway. That was the best spot for coming and going. It was at the end of the outdoor concourse and hidden by a planter with trees that rose beside the broad entrance steps.

Ian had been stealthily pacing the halls for the past two nights and, standing in front of the elevator, he felt in his bones that his father would not return tonight. Despite instructions to stay put, he knew he would have to leave the building. The box of crackers, the peanut butter, and the milk they kept cold outside on a window ledge had been gone since yesterday. Ian didn't know where he would find something to eat, but he didn't dare wait until the town shut down around ten. First, he would need to get a key.

He listened for any sounds of life in the building before he took the elevator. It was a treat he and his dad reserved for when they were certain no one was about. The stairs scared him a little; they seemed to descend into such darkness, to go up into such nothingness. The elevator was fun.

It groaned to a stop in the basement, and he listened when he stepped out. Only the faint sound of the boiler room hummed in his ears. It was around a corner and down a long hallway.

The hall was dimly lit by the exit lights and one safety light. Dozens of small dark offices opened from the many corridors down here. There was one large room with a long counter that had been the traffic violations bureau.

Ian was not afraid of the basement—at least, there was no increase in the wary caution that was part of his waking life, that even accompanied his sleep. No one else lived in the Hall of Justice. Delbert Joe, a short, wild-eyed man, slept outside on the concourse by the hidden door rolled up in a smudged baby-blue blanket. He couldn't be seen from the street. He was harmless enough, Ian's father said, but they avoided him and always entered by a far door when the strange little man was around. Delbert Joe didn't have a key. Nobody seemed to mind that he slept curled in his baby-blue blanket on the cement concourse at the front of the old building. The police left the blanket when they made their sweeps.

His dad had a key. They had found it in a cold chamber off the hot and booming boiler room. Against a wall was a metal cupboard of keys arranged according to some code. There were probably several hundred keys to different doors in the vast building. And, at the bottom of the cupboard, were six master keys on a twined wire.

"One," said his father. "We'll just take one—a master key. That's all we'll need and we're set for the winter, Ian. We don't want anyone missing two keys." *Pull back; stay out of sight; don't leave a trace.* His father's code.

They could get through any door with that key. Ian and his father had explored all the rooms in the building except one great dark, dark room, the Fifth District County Court, that sprawled in the middle of the second floor and in which they couldn't turn on the lights. They had even examined the tunnel bordering the skylight shaft on the second floor, the one above the big circuit courtroom. It was tomblike and soundless. Workmen could crawl out onto a catwalk between panels to clean or repair the glass.

"Stay off the catwalk," his father had warned.

"Your shadow could be seen if the lights came on."

But his father carried the key with him, and Ian knew he now needed a master key for himself.

The boiler room he went through was comfortingly noisy and warm, but the dark chamber beyond made him uneasy. Cold October air seeped in around a door to the outside, bolted shut.

Ian felt for the light switch and the place leaped into light—ugly and bare. There was a refrigerator in one corner, empty but still working; Ian couldn't understand why it was kept running. Out of hope and habit, he opened it. Of course. He knew it was empty. Momentarily he imagined what he wished sat on its shelves—a ham sandwich on a plate. Apple pie. But he had no time for this game now.

The key cupboard was over a gray institutional desk. Its door was slightly open, which surprised Ian. He and his dad had found it closed and had left it that way. Carefully, using one finger at the edge of the door, he opened it. Even the inside of the door was hung neatly with labeled keys— M4-78, M4-79—numbers meaningless to Ian. He felt around the bottom for the master keys, then looked. They were not there. Just a few loose keys. Disappointment crawled along his skin. No master keys. Probably the museum people had taken them. He would have to prop open an outside door to get back in. And risk someone else slipping in or, worse, risk discovery.

Hunger prodded him back to the stairs. He didn't know who might have come back in overhead on the first floor, so he left the elevator where it was. Silently he climbed his way to the main level. He was too hungry to go back up to the second floor to get his backpack, which, normally, he took with him everywhere. It held his comb and toothbrush, three changes of underwear, two clean T's, a dark turtleneck, and two pairs of socks. His father had warned him to always carry his belongings with him or find a place to stow them that he knew he could get back to.

By the stairs was the hidden door, and Ian, using a wad of paper plucked from some debris in a corner, jammed it into the tongue of the lock and tested the door by gently pushing it open and closed. Then he made his way silently to the big entrance foyer that sported four doors with exit bars in the middle. He found one that didn't close completely unless it was really forced. He slipped outside and gently eased it shut. The cold hit him like a blow. He unfolded his Nike cap from his pocket and slipped it on, pulled up the collar of his denim jacket, and jogged down the steps, headed downtown. If he moved fast, he could warm himself—get away from being seen here. He felt hope rise up. He would find food. And he had two doors through which to return to warmth and safety.

◆══◉══◆

The terrible screaming started in the night, and Patient 227 in the semiprivate room off ward four woke up whimpering and moaning. Whenever the screaming began in his head, no matter if he was awake or dreaming, he was back next to that rice field where the new grunt, Ralsky, had fallen into the man trap. Ralsky was still alive and stayed that way for screaming hours with the bamboo spikes sticking up through his body. Would have been merciful if one had gone through his heart. No one could get to Ralsky without getting himself shot, not while they were being peppered with gunfire from a nearby hill. They couldn't even get close enough to put Ralsky out of his misery though he begged for that over and over.

Patient 227 was back lying next to a wounded buddy in a cleft in the ground. Beside him, a row of rice seedlings sprouted green shoots. Even after the firing ceased, they dared not move. Toward evening the screams stopped and Ralsky began talking to people back home: his mom; he had a long argument with his football coach; he talked softly to someone he called Cookie. His voice was hoarse, sometimes rising to a gurgling protest, sometimes filled with sweetness. Once he said "okay" in a reasonable voice. After that he was silent.

"He's taken the train," said Brutus, their sergeant, next morning. No one else wanted to look, but Brute said they owed it to Ralsky and they needed the knowledge of the pit. "Ralsky will help keep you alive. Learn something," he said. So they looked.

Now whenever the screams started in Patient 227's head, he saw the pit with its forest of bloody spikes piercing up through Ralsky's dead body.

The knowledge Brute insisted they draw from the pit along with Ralsky's body built a caution in all the men in the unit, an alertness toward any disturbed ground no matter how cleverly disguised it was. Throughout the war, they made bitter jokes about lessons learned from the dead. How to keep silent as dirt when Stern's laugh was torn from his throat by a bullet. How to spread out during a reconnoiter after a group of five men, clustering for comfort, was killed by a single grenade. They named these lessons for their dead comrades. "Looks like a Ralsky" meant "Careful. Disturbed ground." If you laughed too loudly, you were doing a Stern. If you slept too deeply, you were risking Swartout's dream after Bill Swartout who'd never heard the command to "Boot up and move out." Less than a minute after the order, just as Brute had turned to bark the command again into the bunker, a shell had taken away Swartout's dreams forever.

Patient 227 sat up. He was in a clean bed. The screaming had gone. There was someplace he had to be.

School? Barn chores? It was too dark outside. He would try for forty winks before his mother began calling up the stairs.

Patient 227 lay back down for forty winks in a hospital bed in a semiprivate room on the second floor of the Veterans Administration hospital. He would sleep for forty-two hours, wake up, and remember who he was for a moment. Then the screaming in his head would start all over.

CHAPTER TWO

Food and Sleep

Ian crossed through the middle of a miniature park next to the Hall of Justice. The little park needed tending. Paint peeled from the benches and grass had grown in the cracks of the curving sidewalks. Only six or seven weeks ago, in mid-September, it was warm enough for a few raggedy people to sleep all night on some of the more secluded benches. Now, an old newspaper stirred beneath one of them in the late October wind and Ian shivered, pulling the collar of his jean jacket more tightly about his neck.

On Michigan Avenue, the gleaming glass and steel of modern office structures abutted well-kept, old-fashioned brick buildings. Some of the office windows were still lit. His shoulders hunched against the cold, Ian noticed that Christmas deco-

rations were already being hung from streetlights—
HAVE A GRAND RIVER CHRISTMAS in tinsel and twinkle.
On the streets, shoppers in winter coats strolled,
chatting together. Ian slowed to a stroll, too, blot-
ting out the cold with his mind.

He headed toward the center of the shopping
district, where restaurants huddled in a friendly
glow of lights. You could choose from burger
chains, discreetly toned down from their cartoony
appearance to the Grand River downtown style.
A Chinese restaurant, Hong Kong, reminded
passersby of their newly acquired liquor license.
Lovely smells came from La Potageria, where you
were assured that the soups in Styrofoam bowls
were homemade and the wrapped sandwiches
hearty. The Coffee Plantation served sandwiches,
too, and all kinds of coffee and tea from around
the world. Ian and his father had explored them
all, and when they had a little money, had eaten
sparingly in a few of them.

Sometimes, outside the restaurants downtown,
Ian had noticed that people dumped their food
cartons and bags into the city's tidy disposal containers, which were all decorated with a leaping
fish—the logo of Grand River. Leaping fish were to
be seen everywhere—on doorways and banners
and jackets—"Except in the river," his father had
said. "No leaping fish there, I'll bet. Anymore."

The disposal lid lifted up neatly. You could reach into the plastic liner and retrieve the cartons. If you were in luck, you might find some limp fries or the cold remains of a hamburger. Once Ian had salvaged part of a stacked ham sandwich and a nearly full container of potato soup, still warm. He often dreamed about that meal.

Potato soup on his mind, Ian stopped outside La Potageria.

On this night he was not lucky. No one brought out food to discard. With an eye made sharp by longing, he could see them through the wall of windows, folks seated comfortably in booths, coats shed and pillowed behind them, or perched on tall stools at high round tables. The place was crowded—Thursday-night shoppers taking advantage of pre-Christmas sales. The early darkness made everything in La Potageria seem brighter; his hunger and the cold glorified the view of thick, hot soup spooned happily into people's mouths. The act of chewing became fascinating to him—the swallowing.

Two girls next to the window got up to leave, gathering packages. They were, perhaps, in high school and they were laughing. One of them carried her drink with her, sucking on the straw.

And they were leaving food!

Ian plunged through the door. There was a small line waiting for paid-for food at the counter. He slowed down. "Excuse me." Past the two girls who headed for the door he had entered by. *Stay calm.*

With painful casualness, Ian eased to the place near the window, slipped up onto a stool at the tall round table. In the street outside the window the girls passed by, their faces alight with laughter.

Stay calm. Carefully Ian pulled the plastic bowl toward him. Half full! He dared not leave his find for a clean spoon, so he wiped the lipstick from the one in the bowl with an almost-clean paper napkin. He had nearly finished the contents of the bowl when he realized it was a thick vegetable soup, not potato. But it felt good filling his mouth, warming his throat. There was also part of a sandwich, a half cup of cocoa, and some more of the vegetable soup in another bowl. The girls had left a half dozen small packets of saltines. Ian stuffed them in his jacket pocket. He was beginning to feel warm.

He looked around to see if there was any more abandoned food. Now that his hunger had been appeased, caution seeped back into him. He began to do his invisible trick. It was something his dad had taught him—how to blend with his surroundings; how to become a part of any place. He loosened his jacket. He looked casually around the restaurant as if he were checking for a parent; he assumed a bored expression. He got up, took his empty cup and went for ice and water, which were free. Returning, he noticed a newly vacated booth. He leaned against it, sipping his cocoa-tasting water. He was indeed invisible. No one looked his way. He sat down in the booth. A family must have eaten here. The table was a mess of containers and napkins and crumbs. Perhaps that's why someone had left a tip. He folded the wrapping around the remains of a sandwich and pocketed it along with more crackers and seventy-five cents, half of the busboy's tip, all the while yawning and looking around in a bored, sleepy manner. Seventy-five cents wasn't as good as a buck and a half, but he would leave no traces.

On the way back to the Hall of Justice, though the wind had picked up, Ian felt warmer. He turned his cap backward in a celebration of well-being. His pockets were full of breakfast. The place he returned to was warm. Perhaps his dad would be back. If not, there was always the mirror game, a game he'd invented of combing his hair into different disguises. There were large mirrors in all of the bathrooms in the former Hall of Justice. They gave him a well-lit view of a tall, lean-faced boy with hazel eyes and a thick helmet of dark red hair. If he wet his hair down and plastered it to his head, his face looked long and narrow, like an old-style actor. He could part his hair down the middle and slick the sides back, a fashion he'd recently noted on boys his age. If he squeezed some soap from the dispenser into his hands and ran them through his hair, he could comb the mass up into a peak on top of his head. He could sort it into two peaks or spike it into five. He had discovered different voices for the characters he became, different attitudes. He felt good enough tonight to play the mirror game before he went to sleep. He felt warm enough to withstand rinsing his hair in cold water over the sink.

To keep himself company, he began to pretend he was his father. *Got to get us some blankets, Ian.* Blankets to wrap themselves in for sleeping would make things even better. Ian had begun to feel cold when he slept. And pillows. Pillows would be nice. Except, of course, pillows would mean "unnecessary trappings," as his father called it.

"Keep it simple," his father always said. "Survival minimum."

"I don't really need a pillow," said Ian softly to himself as he crossed through the little park. He would rest his head on his backpack as usual.

Soon I will need gloves though, he thought, and a warmer coat. His father's warm coat was tucked in one of the file bins near the license bureau, but Ian's coat had been way too small last winter. In the spring, they had donated it to the Salvation Army for somebody else. His father had a notion of getting Ian a new warm coat, but Ian didn't know how he planned to do that, so he began to think of ways himself.

Of course, one way was to go into a store without one, preferably on a snowy day, and walk out wearing a new one. A safer, less exciting method was to visit the Salvation Army and see what seventy-five cents would buy. He could wear his father's, but suppose his dad came back while Ian was out? He might need the coat. I'll have to leave a note, thought Ian, with Dad's coat. First, search again for a master key.

There were so many things to take care of that Ian began to worry once more. If his dad wasn't back yet, he would make a list.

In the desk left behind in one of the judge's chambers were loose pens and pencils, paper clips, a bunch of telephone message blanks, and an assortment of partly-used-up legal pads. He had already taken some of the yellow paper to write out invented lessons from Miss Lusk, the third-grade teacher he remembered with longing.

Ian quickened his step, his spirit suddenly filled with purpose. First a list, then he would plan. One: a blanket. Two: a winter coat. Three: gloves. Four: more groceries. Five: laundry. He would wait for his dad, who did the laundry at Suds Yer Duds

Laundromat, a good distance away from downtown. Meanwhile he could wash out underwear in the men's room sink. Dry it in the hot furnace room. Somewhere in the back of his mind, not clear enough to put on the list yet, was getting back to school.

The park side of the Hall of Justice was partially lit by street lamps, and Ian stayed in shadow as much as possible, skirting the corner around to the entrance. Half of the wide steps up to the front doors were cloaked in darkness. On the dark side of the concourse was the door Ian had stuffed with paper. It was the safer of the two entrances he had prepared; he could barely see the door in the shadows.

Turning onto the concourse, he nearly tripped over the bundled shape of Delbert Joe curled there. Was it Delbert Joe? He couldn't be sure. Or was it just a rumpled blanket? Ian bent over in the darkness to inspect the shape. An unpleasant smell rose from the sleeping place. No breath, no movement, the bundle in the blanket was too small to be a person. He nudged it with his foot, then kicked aside the blanket. With growing bewilderment, he bent closer to examine what turned out to be his own backpack.

The back of Ian's neck went cold to his hair roots, and he whirled around to the black shadows by the door.

"Dad?" he asked into the darkness.

The shadows held no one. He picked up his backpack cautiously. Underneath he could make out a half-used legal pad. From the desk inside?

"Dad?" he asked again.

He stood there listening in the shadows. An occasional car went by on Division Street, stopped at the light at Michigan. His arm began to ache and he realized he was holding the backpack up. He lowered it, wrapping his arms around his lumpy belongings. Now the cold bit into him and he had a sudden, strong desire to lie down. He turned and yanked at the door but it no longer opened. Someone must have gone through the door and accidentally or deliberately knocked out the piece of paper stemming the lock's tongue.

He began to shiver uncontrollably. He had never felt so cold. Teeth chattering, he hunched over his backpack and hurried along the concourse. Gone was his wary care to stay hidden. He stumbled to the wide main doors, pulled at the one he had fixed open. It gave way, knocking him off-balance; he staggered, nearly falling into the warmth of the lobby.

Some semblance of caution returned, and after he had caught his breath and stilled the chattering of his teeth, he crept through the secondary doors into the dimly lit hallway. Breathing shallowly, he slipped past the elevator and around the corner to the stairway. He climbed slowly, listening behind him, listening before him, above him in the darkness. The second floor was warmer and he headed toward the room for miniature people—for close walls, sweet low windows, for safety.

Every atom of his sensory system was alert—eyes and nostrils wide, head cocked listening. He sent out invisible antennae from his skin, like feelers on an ant, whiskers on a cat. The second-floor hallway felt empty. Past the doors of the great dark, dark Fifth District County courtroom he crept, heart beating almost audibly. Was he imagining it or did his antennae quiver; had someone slipped into the darkness of that dead courtroom?

Once inside the room for miniature people, he took a breath, exhaled shakily. His chest hurt. It took a few minutes to calm his breathing, to stand up straight. Then he considered how to secure the door. It opened inward, toward the room. Noiselessly, he stepped out into the hallway again. He listened without breathing to the silence before he slipped around the corner to one of the offices and returned with a wooden chair to prop beneath the doorknob, barring the door. But what if his father came? How would he know it was Ian closed tight in the room for miniature people? At the Squirrel's Nest they had had a signal for entry—two long raps on the window followed by three quick taps with a fingernail. Whoever was inside could warn the other away by coughing loudly. The walls were thin as sheets; you could easily hear a cough. What had they been hiding from then? Ian couldn't remember. Was it when his aunt Mildred had been looking for them to take Ian away?

After he had wedged the back of the chair under the doorknob, Ian lay down, backpack beneath his head. He was exhausted but afraid of surrendering to sleep. Turning his face toward the little windows, he closed away all thoughts of the rooms along the darkened hallway, erased the vast floor below and the one below that with its booming furnaces. An array of twinkling holiday lights patterned the windows across the way. He pulled the room in around him like a coverlet.

Sometimes he would put himself to sleep by doing the times tables in his head. He was good at ones and twos, fives and tens. Usually he was asleep before he got to the hard ones. His father had drilled him in all of them as well as in telling time. *You need to think forward and backward; you need to know where you are and what time it is.* He had shown Ian how to know time by the sunlight in different seasons, but Ian preferred the clocks in the Hall of Justice. No guesswork.

Many nights, Ian would prepare for sleep by trying to establish a good dream. He would lie on his back imagining his grandmother's fields, her kitchen, or he would focus on the hallway in his old school and work at walking through the doorway of Miss Lusk's class. He would try to picture his teacher's face, but he had worn that memory so thin that it rarely came to him anymore. Concentrating on her plaid slacks and gray wool sweater as she stood leaning over her desk was easier. He tried remembering her voice. "Class, today Ian has brought his rabbit to school." Miss Lusk had praised his show-and-tell, not just for the rabbit. She had told him, "You have the gift of gab, Ian. You seem to know how to make ordinary things interesting." Sometimes, on lucky nights, he could feel her hand on his shoulder.

Unpleasant memories he tried to keep at bay, but often they burst into his dream plan: Miss Lusk in a coat streaked with rain on the porch of his grandmother's house. His father, inside, kept saying, "Close the door, boy. Close the door." Was that a real memory?

The images kept getting mixed up with what he wanted to dream, and the dreams themselves were never what he planned.

On this night he lay awake listening for sounds outside the door, never expecting to fall asleep. But before long, he drifted off and dreamed vividly without planning anything at all.

CHAPTER THREE

Plaid Lady

His grandmother was bringing sandwiches out to the weathered picnic table at the edge of the apple orchard. An old apple tree, standing apart from the others, spread feathery shade over the benches and table. She has stopped being dead then, thought Ian with relief.

When his grandmother set the tray down on the table, Ian saw there were two steaming bowls of homemade tomato soup. The plate of sandwiches turned out to be cheeseburgers and steak fries.

"Your father's asleep," said Ian's grandmother. She turned her weak, pale eyes to him. "In his old room." Ian looked toward the house. In the back doorway stood a boy with red hair like his own. His grandmother's shadow stretched from the picnic table way down to the door and half covered the boy in the doorway. "He slept past chores," his grandmother said. She sat down at the table and spread a napkin across her lap. She took a sweet pickle from a jar on the tray.

"I'm here, Bams," said Ian. "I can do chores." But he felt helpless, small.

"Tell me one of your stories," said his grandmother. "I'd rather hear a story." Ian could make up good stories.

"Tell me about the apple trees, or a bird, a fish."

But Ian couldn't think of a single story about a tree or a bird or the pond or anything.

"I've come for the boy," said his father from inside the house. Ian turned toward the sound. The boy in the doorway had disappeared along with his grandmother's shadow. He turned back in alarm to the picnic. Bams was lying on the table now, on her back—arms folded across her chest, her shadow tucked in around her.

"My big boy," she said without looking at him. Her lips moved like a nutcracker doll. "Bams's big, smart boy."

"Shut the door," said his father from somewhere in the house.

Ian wanted to get into his room over the dining room. Carefully he climbed the trellis on the side of the house to the window ledge. The window was wide open to let in the spring air. He climbed right in and sat on his little bed.

But he heard someone crying in the attic and he followed the sound up there. His mother was sitting among old newspapers. She was wearing the cheerleader outfit from the photo his grandmother kept on the dresser in his room. His cheerleader mother was crying because she had just read in the newspaper that his father was missing in action. She was crying because her stomach was so big with a baby stretching out the cheerleader sweater, and she was crying because the baby would kill her. But Ian didn't cry because he was Bams's big, big boy. He just had this yawning emptiness, a terrible hollow ache as though someone had taken something from inside him and sealed it with Novocain so his outsides didn't feel anything.

"Murderer," said his cheerleader mama in the voice he had never heard, looking at him with the face he had never known.

"Bams's big boy," said his grandmother. She took the newspaper from his mama.

"Close the door," said his father.

And then Ian was awake, wide awake with his eyes staring up into the dark ceiling in the room for miniature people. His dream, with its oddly mixed times and places, receded, leaving the sound of his father's voice a soft echo in his ears.

He sat up in a rush of gladness. But he stayed quiet, waited for a signal. Then he crept to the door and listened some more—for two long raps, three taps—listened for breathing beyond the door.

Ian knew patience, and it was a long time before he let his breath out slowly. No one was there outside the door. He was pretty sure. Not his father. Not a monster. What time could it be? Now he had to go to the bathroom.

The safest bathroom was down the hall in a judge's chambers. In the public men's room, some-one could be hiding in a stall. What time was it? How long before daylight? He bent and looked out the window; lay down and tried to see the sky between the buildings.

The sky was dark beyond their darker shapes.

No one was lurking outside waiting for him to open the door. Was there?

He listened at the door again. Now he had to go really bad. Outside, the long silence of the hallway seemed to collect behind the door.

"When the demon is on you," his father once said, "you must make your mind cold and clear as ice." When had the demon been on his father? In the war. But where? *Cold and clear as ice.*

Ian quieted his heart, forced his breathing to become slow and even, relaxed his shoulders.

There is no one outside, he told himself. But he took his backpack with him when he opened the door and walked, head up, with measured steps, toward the judge's chambers.

"Never act like a victim," his father had said. But he also warned Ian not to show off and call proud attention to himself. *Never act like a victim—or a target, either.*

No one followed Ian to the bathroom. No one waited for him outside afterward. Then Ian stood in the second-floor chambers looking out of tall windows. It was a different view than from the identical windows below, the tops of trees, more sky. And the sky, Ian could now see, was lightening. Dawn was easing away the night. With the promise of daylight, he knew for certain he was alone in the building.

It wasn't until after Ian had eaten his breakfast crackers and the half sandwich, after he had taken a good long drink from the drinking fountain, that the others began to arrive.

He was on the landing of the north stairway between the first and second floors when he heard a nibbling rattle at the side door, the hidden one. Then an explosive, "Damnit!" He froze, then backed up the stairs into shadow.

It was a woman. He heard her say "All right!" when the door finally opened. There was a sound like boxes or bags sliding across the short corridor, a few hearty curses as she pushed or tugged these weighty possessions to the main hallway. She was oblivious to his presence. He sat on the top step and listened, trying to figure out if she was alone. Later he heard her clumping around below, humming in a loud voice. He thought maybe there was someone else because she held conversations throughout the several hours she was there. Finally he heard, "This phone is costing me a fortune, even if *you* call me, Randy. So get to the point." Ian realized she was carrying a phone around. Once she commented, "This place gives me the creeps."

Later he heard her yelp to someone on the other end, "Dibs on the judge's chambers! There's a desk already there. It's mine!"

She left briefly about midday. Ian was hungry again and was just planning a foray to find food when she returned. He saw her from a window in the second-floor judge's chambers. She had cropped, graying hair, and wore hiking boots and a big red plaid coat. She walked fast with big strides. A very noticeable person. Not a victim but an easy target, thought Ian. She was carrying a paper bag and a coffee container. Lunch. Ian's mouth watered. Suddenly he remembered the cookies from the night before. They were probably still there.

The plaid lady still seemed to have trouble with the key at the side door. "Damnit!" was apparently a natural part of her vocabulary.

Before the door opened, Ian heard another voice greet her. The "damnits" stopped and the woman's voice turned bright and businesslike.

"Good. You're right on time. Can you get this key working? I know it works, but it's a copy so you have to do battle with the keyhole."

When the door finally opened, from his stairway shadow, Ian thought he could distinguish the footsteps of three people.

"You must be Officer Pratt?" the woman was saying.

"Yes, ma'am. This is my foreman, George . . ." They passed below and Ian resisted the impulse to lean out from the shadows and catch a glimpse as they moved toward the main hallway, their voices growing muffled.

Ian strained his ears. Which way were they going once they reached the hall? By the sound, they seemed to be headed toward the circuit courtroom with its vast ceiling—where the cookies might still be.

The eastern sky door was closest, and Ian hurried on noiseless feet to climb the ladder to the roof. Then he crunched across the gravel and entered the steel door above the courtroom ceiling. The great lights had just been turned on, so it was still cold on the walkway.

"The main problem," Plaid Lady was saying, her voice rising plainly to where Ian stood, "is moving the spectator benches."

"Yes, ma'am, they're bolted to the floor underneath."

"Oh, no," moaned the lady.

"Nothing we can't handle," said Officer Pratt. "This group is a good bunch. We've got some experienced builders here."

"In the Sheriff's Work Patrol?" Plaid Lady laughed. "Handpicked, I suppose," she said with sarcastic good humor.

"These men are serving their time productively," said Officer Pratt. "They are all good workers. One of them ran his own construction business. We're using energy and time for the public good that would otherwise be wasted in a cell. It's free to the community. Everybody wins."

"Amazing!" said Plaid Lady. "I'm certainly pleased I found out about you all. When can you start?"

"We'll be here Tuesday morning at eight sharp," said Officer Pratt. "Right, George?"

"Do you always supply cookies?" asked the man called George.

Plaid Lady laughed again. "Those must be from

last night. Surprised the mice didn't get into them. Maybe there're no mice. Old as it is, this building is tight as a drum. Help yourself. They may be a little stale left out like that."

"No, thank you, ma'am," said George. "We'll take doughnuts in the morning though."

How casual their talk of food. Ian knew he would have to leave the building again before he got too hungry. He ran through his mind the doors he might prop unlatched. The front one, through which he had entered during last night's panic, was easy to slip out of its latch. He could also wedge something in the exit door behind the district courtroom. Maybe, just to be on the safe side, he would prop open the side door by the little park on the east side of the building. "CYA," his father had said. "Cover your ass."

"You'll have to store the benches beyond the old library—perhaps in the south hallway," the lady was saying, and Ian could hear them leave the courtroom by one of its side doors.

If they stayed awhile in the south side of the building, Ian might have time to fix two of the north doors for his return. He tried the west sky door and it opened easily. Moving fast and quietly, he clambered down the ladder, slipped down the stairs and into the lobby with its broad expanse of doors. Listening, turning his head, he crept to the entrance he had stumbled through last night. He pushed it gently until it clicked open, then took his hand away. A sliver of cold air was the only evidence the door was caught open.

Back in the main hall, he listened for voices, footsteps, the brush of bodies against the stale air. Apparently the intruders were still on the south side. He would have time to fix another entrance. He sprinted down the hall to the double doors of the circuit courtroom. The right one made a crunch-click as it opened—unavoidable. The noise was like an explosion in his head. He paused, holding his breath. No movement. He closed the door carefully, then hurried down the carpeted center aisle. The stale cookies still sat on the third-row bench, but to take one now would leave a noticeable hole. Later he would have time to make it look like mice had been there—scattering crumbs and such. Now he hurried to the door between the jury box and the judge's bench. "Even a judge," his father had speculated, "has more than one exit." And it was true; the judge's high platform was flanked by two.

Ian pushed into the hallway along the eastern side of the building and hurried through the short foyer to the outside door. There was a real door prop on the floor in the dusty corner, a little wooden wedge. He would leave from this exit.

Outside, he pushed the wedge into the bottom corner of the frame and let the door settle against it. Food was next on the agenda. Then he would think about a coat.

This time he walked ten short and two long blocks to a huge grocery outlet, Horrebs. If you went midday, you could fill yourself with pleasantly proffered samples: slivers of pizza, tiny paper cups filled with warm chicken à la king or green beans almondine, cheese on crackers, squares of toasted raisin bread, inches of crumbly muffins, popcorn, pudding, tasty triangles of pumpkin pie. Today there was crumb cake, raw broccoli and cauliflower with a hot cheese dip, crackers and seafood spread, and finger-sized lengths of chicken teriyaki. Once his stomach was satisfied, though, it was his father he thought about, not a winter coat. Worrying. Where could he be?

His father had been gone four days now—the longest he had ever been away from Ian since they had been together. Once his dad had stayed away overnight and often he was gone the whole day. When he returned he always had something for them: food or money—one time a baseball that they threw to each other up and down the hallway.

Maybe his dad had gotten the awful shivers again and someone had taken him to a hospital. Maybe he had started that swearing and crying and someone had taken him to the nuthouse. Maybe his father would stay away a long time like when Ian was little and lived with Bams. But his dad had often told Ian during the three years they had been surviving together, "We're a unit, boy." And they were.

Ian worried his dad might return while he was out getting food or a coat or a blanket—or watching the kids leaving school. His dad might think Ian had gone for good.

He returned quickly to the Hall of Justice. No cars were parked outside. He listened carefully as he slipped in the entrance he had pegged open. Next time, he ought to leave a clue to be disturbed so he'd know if someone else had used this door.

The building seemed to be empty. Passing through the big circuit courtroom, Ian noticed the cookies were no longer there. But he couldn't waste time on regrets as he hurried, still listening, down the hall. In the judge's chambers on the first floor, he pulled out one of the legal pads. He wrote:

Dear Dad,
We are out of food. I will be back. I am sleeping
on the second floor. Your son, Ian Bayless.

He thought of writing down the time from the clock on the wall but he wasn't sure what day it was. So he just added: *P.S. It is October.* He folded the paper and wrote *Mitchell Bayless* on the outside. It made him feel better, writing his dad's name like that.

Then he realized that his note gave away too much. He wadded it up and stuck it in his pocket to discard later in a safer place. On fresh paper, he wrote:

MB Downtown for food. Otherwise, still here.
Oct. IB

Down below in the basement, in the storage bin with his father's coat, he left the note.

◆══◉══◆

The sheets were clean and he was wearing a clean bed shirt and a part of him wondered how he had gotten there. But he already knew this scene. The rescue unit had finally lifted him from the ambushed hill. He had dragged Will there after stopping up the bloody hole in his stomach with all the bandages from the medkit. He had been worried about leaving a trail of bent grass, traces of their laborious progress to this spot. Where was Will? Where were Skunk and Reefer? Had they airlifted them, too?

Now he remembered clearly waking from a drowned sleep to the sound of the chopper, the grass flattening around them, bits of debris like BBs pelting his face and arms. He had been propped against a rock holding Will in his arms, trying to keep him warm—keep life from leak-

ing out of him. They had to pry his arms from the stiff-ening body. His own body grew cold where Will had been; his leg had begun to throb. Skunk had lost his left hand and a lot of blood, but Reefer had tied off the artery above the elbow before he crept back down the hill to look for others. Skunk had insisted on hanging on to the part of his hand he'd found on the ground. "Sometimes they can put these back on," he kept saying over and over.

Where were Skunk and Will and Reefer now?

Patient 227 brought the room into focus, looking for IV tubes and the pulley holding up his leg in a cast— looking for the row of beds in the field hospital. Knowing the scene.

And it was not the scene.

This was a room with only one other bed—empty. Panic surged up in him from a subterranean well of ter-ror. Will was dead. Skunk had lost half his arm, and Reefer had never returned. He sat up, expecting pain in his leg to match the fear in his head. There was no pain, but the effort left him shaking. Where was he? What had happened? Was this part of another dream? Could he safely awaken?

CHAPTER FOUR

The Girl

He was watching for Plaid Lady. From the tall windows in the second-floor judge's chambers, Ian had a fine view of the parking lot on the west side of the Hall of Justice. With luck, he could see Plaid Lady or anyone else who might be coming to the building—at least from the west. This morning there were early skateboarders, en route to school, practicing in the lot. And there was this girl.

She was just emerging from the little park near the building, a tall girl cuddling down into an oversize tan parka, pushing against a wind he knew was cold. Ian guessed she was sixteen, maybe seventeen. Her strides, crossing the parking lot full of skateboarders, were pigeon-toed and deliberate, as if she were measuring each step. She waved to the skaters, then held up a congratulatory thumb when one guy spun, twisting, off a rickety-looking ramp without losing control of his board. She threw back her head, laughed, but did not stop. Faintly through the window, Ian heard the brief, bright sound of her glee. He didn't see her face, but he liked the way her head had been flung back, the way her hood slipped, the twist of dark hair escaping.

Before she got to the corner of the Hall of Justice, he could tell by the easy lean of her body that she was coming around to the main entrance. He raced to the Assistant Prosecutor's office at the front where windows looked down over the broad steps. The girl was climbing them slowly, two at a time. Then his view was cut off by the building, and he hurried to the north stairway. Plaid Lady was cussing heartily outside the door below and Ian froze, then crept into shadow.

The voice that interrupted Plaid Lady's with a low "G'morning" must belong to the girl.

Plaid Lady yelped, "Ah, there you are. Thank heavens! Here, wiggle this key around in the keyhole until it opens the damn door."

There was a click-click rasp at the door and some pushing. The key finally snapped into place and turned.

"Voilà!" That wasn't Plaid Lady. The voice was bright as an apple, skipping low to high. Peering carefully, Ian saw the tan parka.

"I was afraid I'd have to throw gravel against your window again," said the girl. Her voice was oddly low to hold such cheerfulness. "It's getting cold. Maybe I would've covered myself with that blue blanket over there."

"I'd leave that alone," said Plaid Lady. "Some poor guy . . . It's none too clean. We'll have to get you a key."

She was balancing a bakery box on one arm; her other was wrapped around a grocery bag. She held the door open with her back.

"We'll make you a copy of my copy of a copy of the original key." She gave a hoot of laughter. "You'd get in faster if you jimmied the lock with a hairpin."

The girl picked up a huge restaurant-style coffeemaker where it was sitting just outside the door and, bracing it against her body, began to lug it inside. "Who's gonna drink all the coffee?" she asked and, in the same breath, "Are those doughnuts?"

"Forget it," said Plaid Lady. "These are for the Sheriff's Work Patrol. Coffee and doughnuts. I'm not even opening the box until they get here."

The girl gave an exaggerated whimper of mock distress, but she struggled on out of sight with the coffeemaker. Plaid Lady let the door slam shut.

"That'll go into the district courtroom by my

office," she instructed, following the girl. "Then you can come back here and watch for those guys. Too many people wandering around to leave the doors unlocked. Too many people think they can still pay traffic tickets here, or get a divorce, or sue someone. So you'll have to let in the Sheriff's Work Patrol."

Her voice grew fainter as they moved down the main hallway. "They're convicts, you know."

". . . toiling in the Hall of Justice." The girl's voice. Ian couldn't tell if she was serious or joking, until her vivid laugh cascaded back to him at his shadowy post.

He didn't have long to wait before the girl was back, still hooded inside the parka. He watched her open the door below and peer out. She shut the door, blew her breath against its window. Wrote something in the cloudy spot. Wiped it out. She opened the door again and leaned out. Shut the door. Heaved a sigh and slumped against the wall, her face hidden by the hood.

"Unhhh." A frustrated groan issued from the hood. "Boring. Boring." She turned again to the window in the side door. "Come on-n-n, work patrol," she pleaded. "Come on-n-n, convicts. Come on-n-n, worker bees." She straightened up and stretched. "The queen bee waits, trapped in her golden cave."

Ian strained his head out of the shadows, hoping to catch a glimpse of her face.

"Come on before I eat all your doughnuts." Then she stood silently, arms down, as if listening or praying.

She paced. Once she said aloud to the empty hallway, "Why do I need two jobs, Mom?" She paced some more. She faced the hallway again and said indignantly, "I am *not* a teenage dropout. I just don't want to waste the eighteenth year of my life—the *only ever* eighteenth year of my life—in that dreary high school."

Ian was startled. Was she that old? Eighteen? Or did that eighteenth-year stuff mean she was not yet eighteen? He figured in his head. You become one year old after you have lived one year. So this girl was seventeen. She didn't like school. She had two jobs.

"That honor student stuff is junk, Mom; the only good thing was the trip to Holland and the Russian student exchange." The girl leaned her forehead against the wall. Her muffled voice rose. "I don't *care* about the senior prom, Mother. I don't like those jock-jerks in their letter sweaters. I have nothing to say to the *duuh* rah-rah girls in their designer sweats." She emphasized this last by hiking up her dragging jeans.

A banging sound, someone at the front

entrance, interrupted her monologue. She hurried around the corner to the main hallway, hollering, "I'm coming. Don't go away. I'm almost there."

Ian longed to see her face and tracked her movements when, after she had let in the Sheriff's Work Patrol, she wandered through the building below opening and closing doors. What was she looking for, he wondered, grateful that he and his father left no traces. He slipped down the glass-enclosed west stairway on the park side of the building and through the door to the south corridor, where he thought he might be able to catch a glimpse of her.

This was the warmest side of the building. Pausing just down from a big room with a marble floor and great windows—one he liked because of its view of Michigan Avenue and its warmth—he could hear her moving there, then a long silence. So close to her he dared not breathe.

It would be safer, he thought, to slide quietly into the dark room beside him. The lights there were controlled by a special key so he would be in no danger of discovery. But the door made a loud click when he opened it, and for a moment he froze, then slipped inside. He could hear her as she hurried out of the big room and away up the corridor. Had she heard him? Had he frightened her?

He waited. Held the door open a crack. Listened. Then he slipped out, down the corridor, and climbed back to his stairway post, where he watched as the workmen began their noisy activity. The girl had gone where he couldn't see.

In the space of a morning, Ian followed the activity of a platoon of men in fluorescent red vests as they tore out the spectator benches and wooden dividers in the vast circuit courtroom and the smaller district one. He could tell from his second floor which room they were in by the sounds of pounding and ripping. The smell of dust and coffee drifted up.

Ian had several observation posts. One was in the shadows on the second floor at the top of the north stairway from where he had observed Plaid Lady and the girl when they entered. If he leaned discreetly over the railing, he had a brief but clear vision of anyone who entered below. Momentarily, he could see the tops of their heads, their shoulders, and their feet as they stepped out walking toward the main hallway; he could hear their voices clearly. The men in fluorescent vests came and went. A bald man with a clipboard clasped against the chest of his overcoat strode beneath him. Plaid Lady clomped in and out with boxes of stuff, from her car, Ian assumed.

And there was the girl. With her big parka now

removed, he could see she had long, straight almost-black hair, the part like a white line drawn in the middle of her head, a twin shine on either side. Her slow, deliberate way of walking, as if her feet were heavy, fascinated Ian. The bottoms of her jeans, as she stepped forward, were loose, half covering her feet.

There was the ever-present danger of being discovered at this post, but he preferred it to the rooftop hut over the great circuit courtroom, where he couldn't see anything and the sounds of pounding and tearing, muffled voices, and occasional shouts teased him with the impression of strenuous activity. The policeman he remembered as Officer Pratt was often in this room, chatting easily with the workmen. The Sheriff's Work Patrol, Ian thought.

Spying from the roof, from the windows, and the stairwell of the second floor, from the glassed-in exit stairs on the west side of the old building, Ian followed the activity of the Sheriff's Work Patrol as it dismantled benches and dividers in the smaller courtroom next to Plaid Lady's office. Sounds told him when the men were lifting and carrying heavy things, benches probably. From the unfamiliar drafts of cold air that cut through the hallway, Ian assumed that many of the outside doors were propped open so the workmen could maneuver in and out with equipment and tools.

Around noon, from the stairway post, Ian saw the girl with the almost-black hair leave, wearing her parka. She returned a short while later juggling white carryout sacks that held what Ian's nose told him, when she struggled through the door, was soup—minestrone? Maybe tomato. His mouth juiced up, thinking of La Potageria's potato soup. His last meal had been Horrebs' free samples again. He dared not desert the warmth in his building now, though it would be easy to slip out along with workmen and helpers and folks looking for the new Hall of Justice. He was worried that everyone might just finish up while he was out "hunting," as his father called it, and close all the doors securely when they left.

Other people came and went, purposeful people, men and women with briefcases or notebooks. Ian saw them from a second-floor window. Occasionally a pedestrian entered the building, reappeared, hesitated, then headed east—to the new Hall of Justice, thought Ian, to pay a traffic ticket or something.

Later on he saw Plaid Lady and the girl lug a large easel down the wide entrance steps and station it there at the foot—a sign of some kind, from the way they stepped back and studied it. He was curious to know what information the sign carried, but he could check that later. Now he hurried to the staircase to watch them return, his urgency to see the face of the girl with the almost-black hair propelling him.

But it was impossible to see her face from the shadows at the head of the stairs. Plaid Lady was howling in an outraged voice, ". . . and two of the urinals in the men's room won't flush, and we can't turn on the lights in either of the rest rooms and I can't get city maintenance on the phone . . ."

The girl murmured sympathetically. "I could keep trying to get through to them," she offered. Her voice was low and measured.

"No, you'd be too nice to them, Jean," said Plaid Lady. "You need lessons in outrage." He hadn't seen her face, but now he knew her name. Jean. He liked the way she spoke, in a low, careful way. Jean.

The Sheriff's Work Patrol finished shortly after lunch.

When everyone else left in the late afternoon, the building rang with silence. It took awhile, in the quiet, for Ian's ears to hear the creak and whisper of small sounds he had formerly been guided by.

Plaid Lady's office in the judge's chambers had big windows that overlooked the skateboard lot. It was a spacious room flanked by a storeroom on one side and a windowed office on the other. In the wake of quiet after everyone had left, Ian visited Plaid Lady's office in search of the master key. The door was locked, but Ian knew if you went through the district courtroom nearby and out the jury door at the rear, you could work your way through a couple of rooms to a back door into Plaid Lady's office.

Kind of dumb, thought Ian, like locking a car but leaving the windows down. Of course, neither Plaid Lady nor Jean knew the building very well.

Ian stopped in the district courtroom at the counter in front of the judge's bench to examine the open doughnut box. Two whole doughnuts and a broken one remained. There had been so much chaotic activity that day he felt safe eating it all and leaving the box where it was. There was lukewarm coffee in the coffeepot and a jar of creamer with little striped sticks for stirring. He didn't even have to be careful of crumbs, and he allowed himself one of the clean crockery coffee cups. Now he could hold off thinking about food until he had searched for a master key.

With his hunger calmed, Ian continued to Plaid Lady's office. She had taken over the desk where Ian used to find paper and pencils. A laptop computer and small printer now sat on the side extension. The desktop itself was neat; an upright file holder filled with folders sat on one side. A heavy, old-style telephone looked like a toy tank in the middle.

Ian opened the center drawer. A pile of business cards and torn scraps of paper with names and phone numbers slid into disarray and Ian hastily reassembled them, checking to see if they had been in alphabetical order, then spent ten minutes alphabetizing them just in case. Pens, pencils, and stick 'em notepads littered the rest of the drawer. No keys here. He opened the little top drawer on the left. More files and an envelope that clinked heavily as he lifted it. Keys! His throat tightened and he sucked in his breath with disbelief and hope.

--◦◦◦◦--

Patient 227 slept most of the time, sometimes jerking involuntarily. When he awakened, he lay in a colorless stupor only vaguely aware of the occasional movement of nurses around him. When he slept, he dropped to great depths.

Now the dream was a new one. Not the death pit. Not the prisoner-of-war camp or watching Lieutenant Brydges sink deeper and deeper into a depression no one could reach him through; not the code signals whisked out with a broom in the treeless courtyard, a code that, for some terrible reason, he could no longer decipher—whisk, shhrr, whisk, shhrr-shhrr. And everything depended upon the message—what to tell under torture; what had already been told. Lies. Truths. Whisk, shhrr, shhrr, whisk. Not any of the old dreams.

In this dream, he was walking—though then it seemed like flying—over a green expanse of field and hills. He could see far away, as from a great height. Someone waiting for him in a familiar place. Beyond the next mountain. Not his mother. He couldn't remember who it was, or where it was. Only that this person needed the key he carried in his right pants pocket. He flew on. He kept reaching into his mind for the sound of this person, a name, a name. It was not a nightmare name. It was a warm name, familiar as a kitchen porch.

When Patient 227 woke up, he tried to trace a nagging sense of loss by sending his mind like a hound dog on its trail.

CHAPTER FIVE

The Coat

Oddly enough, the very first key he tried in the keyhole of Plaid Lady's office worked. There were eleven keys, but only one other worked there, too. To his simple satisfaction, the two keys matched when placed together. He tried them successfully in other locks. The real test came when he fitted them into the outside doors, where they also worked. He felt light-headed with power. Two master keys! Then he caught himself. He must minimize his traces. Could he safely take even one key? His father said you couldn't have keys to government buildings copied. They all carried the warning UNLAWFUL TO DUPLICATE in tiny letters. You had to have special permission to get them cloned.

Then he looked at the outside of the key envelope and discovered, scrawled in a hurried hand:

identify (master?). Did Plaid Lady write that? Back in her office, he checked the list of phone numbers she had jotted down and several notes beside her computer. Same hurried handwriting as on the envelope. She always printed the first word in a line—and her *m*'s looked like *n*'s.

So, she hadn't found out yet where these keys went. She didn't know there were two masters and she probably hadn't counted the keys. He hoped. That was a chance he'd have to take.

Keeping one master, he slid ten keys back into the envelope. He resisted the faint urge to tag the other master key for Plaid Lady since he'd taken so much trouble identifying it. But, other than taking the one key, he left no obvious traces.

He felt so elated that he took chances later in his search for food. He visited the Coffee Plantation pretending to look for an uncle and managed, as he was leaving, to lift an entire sandwich from a table, where it sat with a fresh cup of foamy cappuccino. The dining customer was probably in the rest room. Surprise! thought Ian, choking on a chuckle as he headed toward the bus stop. His own daring tickled him. He kept one hand pressed against the sandwich he had stuffed inside his thin jacket. He would eat it when he could safely call it his own. Meantime, a coat was necessary; he would spend the money to get to the mall.

So heated was he with excitement over the acquisition of the sandwich, he barely noticed the cold as he waited on the windy corner for the bus.

As it turned out, he didn't need to use any of his scarce funds for the ride. He mounted the bus right behind a mother with several kids. Lots of people were getting on. The bus driver never noticed. Only the mother looked at him, worried.

"Aren't you cold?" She had just squeezed into a seat with her children.

"I left my coat . . . at the mall," he mumbled. "I'm going back for it."

"Hope it's still there," said the mother doubtfully.

Ian mumbled some more, hurrying to the rear of the bus. "Yeah. I'll find it."

His warm high had deserted him and now, inside the heated bus, he began to feel cold. He remembered with longing the foamy cappuccino steaming in its cup on the restaurant table.

Once he sat down, it occurred to him that the mall might not be the best place to "find" a coat. He comforted himself with his sandwich, munching in the backseat. It turned out to be a ham and cheese with the sweet tang of a mustard he didn't recognize and some funny, hair-thin, green bushy stuff piled inside. It was delicious.

When he reached the mall, he eased in among

holiday shoppers. The vast place was crowded—the stores were crowded, the ice-cream shop was crowded, the large picnic-style eating area attached to six different restaurants was crowded—and people were leaving food on the tables. Ian had dessert. Twice. He gobbled down a dish of melting chocolate ice cream and then a barely-cut-into strawberry crepe.

Many people, he noticed, didn't have their coats with them. They had checked them near the information booth. A pretty girl stood behind a desk at the circular enclosure where shoppers' coats were hanging.

He had been focusing on a new coat. It hadn't occurred to him to think of a used one. He stepped up to the pretty girl.

"That's my coat," he told her pointing at a puffy tan quilted jacket that looked warm. "My mom's in Penney's and we have to go. She has the ticket."

The girl smiled and got the jacket for him. "Have a good evening," she said, blessing him with another smile. "It's cold out there."

Ian walked away, the girl's smiling face following him. She was so nice—so unsuspecting. He felt himself grow small.

The coat was roomy and padded. There were gloves in the pocket. It had a hood, lined with soft wool. It weighed down his arm, bulky and foreign.

He went back to the coat-check desk.

"This is the wrong coat," he told the pretty girl.

"Oh, I'm sorry," she said smiling some more. "Which one is it?"

Ian hesitated. "I think my mom has it," he said finally. "I forgot. My mom has it."

He was rewarded by the deepening of her smile. "Have a good evening," she said again, and turned her smile to a man with a little boy on his shoulders.

My mom, thought Ian, walking away. *My mom.* He had liked the soft sound of it in his mouth. He went into Bickford & Goss, a men's and boys' clothing store. He would ask the clerk, "Is my mom here?"

Two boys and their mother were looking at coats. The oldest, a heavy, fat-cheeked boy, was pouting as his mother held up a hooded gray coat with a red lining.

"You don't know anything," said the boy to his mother. "You have terrible taste."

"This is warm," said the mother. "It's winter."

"I want a Chicago Bull's coat," said the boy angrily. "I hate that coat. It sucks. Nobody wears coats like that. I want an army coat like in the Second World War."

Ian couldn't see what was wrong with the coat. It did look warm. He also couldn't see why the boy needed a new one. He was already wearing a heavy navy coat that still fit.

Moving in close to the rack of coats, Ian spied a sturdy khaki one and reached for it. In his head, he heard himself tell the salesgirl, "My mom is meeting me . . ."

"That's too big for you," said the pouting boy, snatching the khaki coat from Ian. "This is more what I had in mind." He waved the coat toward his mother.

Ian stood still, annoyed and surprised. He didn't like this kid. He was a bully. He was rude to his mother. He didn't need a coat.

The bully kid's mother barely noticed Ian. She was frowning. Then she sighed. "Well, try it on."

The bully kid wiggled out of his navy coat and let it drop to the floor, where he left it.

For a minute or two, Ian watched the boy pose in front of the mirror with his mother hovering near, the little brother whining to go home.

"Will you shut up!" snarled the bully kid to his brother.

Ian flashed a glance around him, then picked up the navy coat from the floor and wandered casually into another aisle, cut out to the mall proper, then ducked into Penney's. In the big department store, he put on the coat and made his way to one of the main exits. The coat was roomy but the sleeves were a bit short for Ian's long arms and the bottom only covered the tops of his lanky legs. It was still warm from the bully kid. It smelled faintly of pizza.

This time he paid for the bus trip back downtown. An envelope inside the coat had five crisp ten-dollar bills in it and a card that said: *To the Birthday Boy from Aunt Karen.* Birthday Bully, thought Ian. Rich Birthday Bully. He would probably not even miss his navy coat.

Ian didn't think his father would approve of his survival methods. First, he shouldn't have taken the tan coat back no matter how nice and trusting the coat-check girl had been. *Do what you have to do when you have to do it and don't look back.* Once in the war, his father had killed a teenage boy. "Protect your life," said his father.

How then to explain this satisfied feeling Ian had as he sat, bundled in navy wool, on the bus while the lights of Grand River blinked comfortably by him? People got on and off the bus. Warm inside the navy coat, he felt like them, a boy going home to supper, homework, TV, and a bed with a real mattress. He had a coat; he had money; he had a key. He was not hungry.

When he got back to the Hall of Justice, it was not empty. As Ian came in the back door at the top of the wheelchair ramp, he saw that lights were on in the circuit courtroom. He heard voices. He hesitated in the doorway, then figured fast. He could creep quietly down the back hall behind the courtroom to the south corridor, down that hall, past the marble floor room, the holding cells, and empty offices, and out the west door. There he could climb the glass-enclosed stairway that rose against the outside of the building. No risk being seen in the dark. But as he hurried noiselessly past the jury room, the door at the other end of the courtroom suddenly opened and light shot through. He eased quickly into the nearest door, the jury room, ran to a window, and waited behind a dusty floor-length drape. Voices filtered in from the hall—men's voices, one pitched high with excitement, the other low. When they grew faint, Ian left his hiding place, opened the door, and listened. They seemed to have gone down the south corridor, the one he had been heading for. He slipped out and stood quietly, still listening.

He heard them enter the courtroom again from a distant door. "This is the exact center of the room. I've walked it off," the low voice said.

"But it doesn't look like the center, don't you see?" said the other man. His voice was hurried and urgent. "There are those splendid vaulted windows that throw the illusion off."

Then the men seemed to be walking around

inside, and Ian followed his earlier plan of using several hallways to get to the outside staircase which would take him to the second floor—his home—the backpack he had hidden beneath a broken desk, and the room for miniature people. He felt little concern about the two men below, but he would secure his door anyway. Tonight he would sleep under the navy coat. Tomorrow he would go to the Coffee Plantation and *pay* for waffles with bananas and maple syrup.

CHAPTER SIX

Traces

As it turned out, Ian decided to wait for breakfast. Early the next morning he observed, from his stairway post, the two men he was sure had been there last night. They had a master key. They let themselves in before Plaid Lady arrived. One was a movie star–looking guy, tall with curly blond hair; the other wore a sort of spy hat with a wide brim that shadowed his eyes. They came in and out at various hours during the day. A few times, they conferred with Plaid Lady.

Once the pair stood just inside the door by Ian's stairway examining a sheaf of blue-tinted paper they had unrolled and were holding open against the wall. Movie Star Guy had an excited voice that tumbled over itself.

"We'll have a center focal point," he said. "An

icon." He pointed to the top of the plan. "Right in the middle of the space." His arm waved, embracing air. "It will anchor the space, pull the room together."

He has the gift of gab, thought Ian. Spy Hat kept nodding, listening quietly.

"I have sketches in the car. When is boss lady Neary getting here? I've thought it out. We can use some of the spectator benches, the long ones—upend them—as supports for the icon. Standing on end, they'll be tall enough to nearly reach the ceiling."

Spy Hat seemed to agree with it all.

"And red! I see lots of deep red. When did you say Neary is coming? She has got to okay the sketches before we can start."

Movie Star Guy wore a tool belt that sheathed a hammer, scissors, measuring tape, and a big staple gun, each in its own pouch. The yellow leather of his tool belt matched his leather boots. He wore little half-moon spectacles that sat like a decoration atop his head; the blue rims were the same shade as Movie Star Guy's soft-draped sweater.

Sometimes the pair stood outside the building and looked up at it. Spy Hat carried the rolled-up sheaves of blue-tinted paper, which he often unrolled and which the two of them studied together.

Ian followed them, moving from stairway to window, back to the stairway, to another window. Their voices led him.

They went up to Ian's roof and took measurements. They climbed out a window onto the balcony over the entrance and took more measurements. Ian was too curious to leave the building just now. He felt alert and powerful, hidden from these men, quick on silent feet, knowing the terrain this pair was studying.

He was at his stairway post when Jean came strolling in late, yawning, and asked if anyone wanted her to get lunch for them. Ian's hunger was no longer desperate. He knew he could leave when he had to. He knew he could purchase food. He could get back in. He would like to buy Jean some potato soup. He felt giddy and a little nuts. Take her to lunch. The money envelope was still in the pocket of the navy coat, *his* navy coat. He had stowed it with his backpack under a broken desk in an office near the room for miniature people.

Ian watched from the top of the stairway as Spy Hat gave Jean some money and his order. ". . . one of those walking tacos and a coke." Movie Star Guy just shook his head and said, "No thanks," then hurried away toward the main hallway, unsheathing his measuring tape as he went.

Ian was no longer eager for waffles with

bananas. What was a "walking taco"?

It wasn't long before he found out. He tracked the two men through the building for a short while. Movie Star Guy discovered the vast room with the marble floor and ecstatically claimed it as his "studio."

Ian was back at his stairway post in time to find Jean struggling with a key in the lock, her arms around a large paper bag. He steeled himself against the impulse to run down and open the door for her. When she finally got in by herself, the aroma of spicy meat, tomatoes, and the sweet bite of onions drifted up the stairwell to where he had been keeping himself in shadow. His mind added crisp taco shells holding a bed of shredded lettuce. His mouth watered.

Before Jean reached the main hallway, he could hear Plaid Lady holler, "Take lunch into the big courtroom, Jean." Judging from the trail of voices and the food smell, they were headed to the circuit courtroom.

Ian hastened to the small alcove that housed the ladder to the sky door. He would be able to hear well from the hut on the roof. He would be able to smell the food.

Scurrying across the roof gravel, he arrived on the steel grating in time to hear Plaid Lady's voice.

"A couple of strange things," she was saying.

Her voice hollowed ominously. "Strange things."

The bag rustled. The smell of food rose faintly up to Ian.

"Yum," said Jean, and then she asked politely, "What strange things?"

"Oh, you've noticed, too?" It was Movie Star Guy's intense voice, so near that Ian, startled into fear, nearly fell from the grating.

He took a breath, calmed himself. The man must be on some kind of ladder or something, up near the ceiling.

"There *are* a few strange things," continued Movie Star Guy. "I found the roof hatch open yesterday morning. I closed it, but it was open again last night."

"Whoooooh," exclaimed Jean. "A mystery guest. That's shivery!"

"What have you noticed, Sam?" A man's voice, thoughtful, a listening person, thought Ian. It must be Spy Hat. Who was Sam?

But it was Plaid Lady who spoke. "I was the last person to leave yesterday, around four, four-thirty—you've got cheese on your chin, Jean—and I locked my office door. I never thought to lock the little courtroom next door—and I know I *didn't* lock it because I went through it to get my coat in back. The door was open then." There was a long, waiting pause.

"This morning, *that door was locked.*" The silence following this statement was heavy with significance.

"Well," said Jean thoughtfully, "you could have locked it as a reflex and not remembered it. You say you are running around like a headless chicken with this job."

Yes, agreed Ian silently. Thank you, Jean. Now he remembered locking it—almost a reflex. Dumb. But he had other worries. Had he forgotten to close the sky door, the hatch as Movie Star Guy called it? Forgotten twice?

"No, I'm sure . . ." Plaid Lady's voice trailed off. She seemed to be looking inward at her memory. "But," she continued slowly, "there's this other thing. It might be nothing. But when I was looking through my ha-ha 'telephone-book'—you know, those scraps with my phone contacts on them?"

Jean laughed. "Telephone book—otherwise known as Useful Small Pile of Scraps."

"They were *alphabetized*," continued Plaid Lady. "The scraps of paper and while-you-were-out notes were in alphabetical order by last names. I know I didn't do that, even accidentally. I keep them in their order of importance, whomever I call the most." She sighed. "You didn't alphabetize my phone numbers, did you, Jean? It was *not* a good deed. Just thought I'd let you know."

"No," said Jean laughing. "I wouldn't dare touch your Useful Small Pile."

"Well, nothing's missing," said Plaid Lady with a sigh. "This place is making me paranoid, I guess." She gave a feeble laugh. "I'll be glad when it's transformed—*if* it's ever transformed. I'll be glad when we rename it—*if* we ever rename it."

"We've got a name!" cried Jean. "Mom came up with it last night."

She seemed delighted to be the bearer of good news.

"So, are you going to tell us?" asked Spy Hat.

"Well," said Jean, dragging out the information teasingly, "she said we've got to get people to stop thinking of this building as the Hall of Justice. She said our sign outside is not doing it."

"That's right," said Plaid Lady. "They're still showing up to pay tickets and get marriage licenses. I keep finding people wandering around whenever the doors are left unlocked."

"Mom says we've got to retrain everybody's thinking," said Jean, "and you all know that's something my mother is really good at." Jean paused. "Mind control."

Everyone laughed. Movie Star Guy's laugh startled Ian again with his closeness. His voice came from directly under Ian. "If anyone can retrain people's thinking about a huge old building that has been in downtown Grand River forever, it's your dynamite mother, darlin'."

So, thought Ian, Jean's mother is the Lady Leader, the one Movie Star Guy calls boss lady Neary.

"You don't want to know what the new name is?" asked Jean in a pouty voice. There was a chorus of "yesses."

"Mom will want to tell you," said Jean, "but I will! You have to pretend to be surprised when she gives you the big news. Okay?" Jean didn't wait for an answer. "ARTlift," she cried. "The new name. One word, but with *art* in caps. ARTlift. Get it? Lift. Kites. Art."

Her voice tripped around and jiggled, and Ian peered in vain through the frosted glass panels, imagining her dancing about in the space below.

"Bravo!" shouted Movie Star Guy. His voice was no longer so close to Ian. He must have climbed down. "I can see the typeface now—a great scrawl of silver letters: ARTlift!"

"Oh, yes!" cried Jean. "And you're to design a fantastic logo, John David—a giant logo to go on top of the building. Everyone will see it. Everyone will think: 'ARTlift.' They'll be curious. They will want to visit. No one will think: 'Hall of Justice.' No one will come for a court hearing." Jean's voice was triumphant. "ART-lift," she said clearly, spitting out the two syllables like separate seeds. "ARTlift. One word."

"Hey!" said Plaid Lady. She sounded pleased. "ARTlift, huh? Well, that helps. Your mother is a cool article." A food bag rustled like a period at the end of a sentence.

"Back to work," mourned Jean.

"No matter what the clock on the wall says," continued Plaid Lady, "city maintenance should be coming in about ten minutes, and the cleaning people I hired yesterday will be here, too."

In the distance, the phone rang. "Finish your lunch and go wait by the main entrance to let them in, Jeanie. I'm still keeping all the doors locked until we get this place jumpin'."

Ian left the roof, careful to close the sky door. I must keep a closer watch on every action, he told himself. *Leave no traces.* And he had things to mull over. Two names. John David. Was that Movie Star Guy? And Sam. Who was Sam? He resumed his second-floor post at the north stairway, thinking about the clocks. That's why he always seemed ahead of time when he went outside. The Hall of Justice clocks were still on daylight saving time.

There was only one guy from city maintenance and, Ian noticed, he had a key. He let himself in and was hauling a ladder. Jean followed him to the main hallway with information. "The center chandelier has three lights out, and the two side ones have only a bulb or two working."

In a few minutes, Ian heard a lobby door click. Jean? Then he heard one of the exits in the main bank of doors open and slam shut. She must be waiting outside for the cleaning people Plaid Lady had mentioned. And she had probably locked herself out—unless she knew about the door that didn't close properly. In order to see her, Ian went into the Assistant Prosecutor's office overlooking the main entrance.

It was apparently too cold to sit on the steps outside but warm enough for Jean to stand in the sun, and she was leaning into the railing with her parka unbuttoned. Her almost-black hair was cradled in back by the lowered hood but fell forward on either side of her face. Ian had never gotten a good look at her face.

She began to pace and talk to herself. Ian sensed her impatience. What was she saying? She stopped and put her hands on her hips, her big parka winging out on either side. She was having a serious argument with someone. Her mother again? She raised her arms, flung her head back, and, before Ian moved back in alarm from the window, he caught a glimpse of her full face for the first time.

It happened in an instant. Her head dropped,

then did a double take—looking back up directly into his window, as if checking for something she thought she'd seen there. He was safe from view and he carried in his mind the image of the pale and pretty face—the eyes very dark and wide, brow furrowed with discontent, the lower lip caught by her teeth. Why was a lovely girl with almost-black hair and a warm parka—a girl who had just eaten all the tacos she could want—so full of displeasure?

CHAPTER SEVEN

The Transformation

"Get the city to fix that door!" The Lady Leader, Jean's mother, was annoyed. She and Plaid Lady were standing by the side door beneath Ian's stairway post.

"We're liable for any damage, even if we don't do it ourselves. Even if it's teenage vandals." The Lady Leader had just come in, unannounced, by opening one of the main doors at the entrance, the one that didn't close properly. Ian was sure he had checked it carefully last night. Perhaps one of the cleaning workers had exited that way. Perhaps Jean had left it ajar this morning when he had been listening to the carpet people as they ripped and pounded in the circuit courtroom. He wondered if Jean, too, had discovered the special trick for using this door. Could she, too, get back in without using a key?

He hadn't seen the tall girl since morning, and he assumed she was in Plaid Lady's office. Earlier, from the hut on the roof, he'd heard Movie Star Guy instruct Jean to make phone calls to locate materials for him, a task that, Jean told the designer, made her sleepy.

"Use your ingenuity," said John David. "See how much of the stuff you can get for us free. This is a nonprofit enterprise. It's for the public good. We have a budget so tiny you'll probably use it up on the phone calls."

"Will businesses do that?" asked Jean. "I mean—just give us stuff? Why would they?"

"For the public good," said Movie Star Guy John David. "Really, lots of people want to help. Like all these lovely volunteers. You can sweeten the pie for those who hesitate. Tell them that donors' names will go on a plaque just inside the door. Tell them their names will be listed in our press releases. Invite them to a private members-only reception. Tell them you'll pick the stuff up in your mother's car."

"Hey! All right!" said Jean. "It's done."

But later that morning, standing at the door beneath Ian's stairway, he heard her say to her imaginary person, "I hate sitting at that desk all day. It's like a prison." Then she leaned her head against the door window. Bumped her brow against the pane a couple of times. "Where is this all going? What am I doing?" she grumbled softly to no one, to the imaginary person.

Over the next few days things really jumped—except for the city maintenance guy, who, Ian had observed, moved slower than anyone he had ever seen. Even when Jean ran through the halls yelling that one of the toilets had overflowed and you would have thought he'd be stepping pretty quickly, he meandered after her with a wrench and a couple of mops as if he were going fishing.

Gradually, the first floor of the old Hall of Justice took on a sheen. The cleaning people were everywhere. Floors were disinfected, scoured with a bristle brush machine, mopped dry, and waxed until they shone. Ian watched, somewhat dismayed, from a window while Jean spent a lot of time laughing on the front steps with some guy on the cleaning staff who, despite the bitter November cold, was wearing only a T-shirt with his tight jeans.

Workers carried rolled-up red weather rugs through the main entrance. Ian heard the slap and squeal of rubber as the rugs were arranged in front of the entrance and lobby doors and down the hallway. Walls were washed and the main hallway painted. The rust was cleaned from the public toilets, and they eventually all flushed efficiently. Graffiti in the bathroom stalls was painted over. Dust and cobwebs disappeared. A new brightness issued from what Ian could see of the main hallway; he supposed all of the chandelier bulbs were now working, their domes cleaned. Doors stopped squeaking. The smell of disinfectant and paint rose to the second floor. The carpet people, after ripping up the faded, dust-heavy old rugs in the courtrooms and some of the other rooms, prepared the floors and put down new carpeting—a dark, royal-looking red.

Ian remembered hearing Movie Star Guy tell Plaid Lady and Jean's mother, "Red! The ARTlift colors are red with touches of black and silver."

Because Movie Star Guy and Spy Hat sometimes came to the second floor with the rolls of blue-tinted paper to look and talk and measure, Ian often had to hide quickly. He was never sure, at first, which area they would visit. In the beginning, they seemed to be exploring, the same way he and his father had. When he heard them on the stairs or in the elevator, Ian had to take a wild guess and jump behind a door or slide into a utility closet. After a while, their visits developed a pattern. They were mainly concerned with the windows that opened out over a balcony above the main entrance, and they also climbed to the roof. They dragged thick orange extension cords with them, lowered them from windows, slid them under doors, hauled them up the wall ladder to the roof, taped them to floors, tested them in wall sockets. They brought up boxes of Christmas lights and stored them in the little sky door alcove.

One night Movie Star Guy and Spy Hat stayed late and hung something red outside from the roof. He heard them call to each other, Spy Hat on the ground and Movie Star Guy above. Ian could partially see, from a window, the flapping of color. After the pair left, Ian slipped downstairs and outside to get a real look. It was almost dark. Suspended between the high windows, four red banners reached from the roof to the ground. *ARTlift* was scrawled in black and silver across the top of each banner. More banners decorated the other sides of the Hall of Justice.

Ian recalled the designer saying, "We're gonna stop traffic with the look of this place." And, indeed, Ian noticed that the traffic on Division Street was slowing down even though the light was green.

Movie Star Guy and Spy Hat often came back when they'd finished dinner. One time they took the Christmas lights up to the roof and Ian heard them crunching around on the gravel. Another night they strung lights in the bare limbs of trees that sat in planters by the main entrance. Sometimes they didn't go home until after midnight.

Ian had to be more cautious if he left the building at night. He tried to escape for his grocery shopping during the day. Chances of running into Birthday Boy on a school day while wearing the navy coat were slight. Free samples at Horrebs were vital to stretching out his money, and he had to figure carefully how and when to return with food supplies. During the day, he could pretend to be looking for the Hall of Justice. "I need a copy of my birth certificate," he thought he would explain if questioned. So many people were working at the Hall of Justice, he only had to be careful not to run into Plaid Lady, who seemed to check everything, or Jean, who seemed curious as a child. Otherwise, he could slip in and out unnoticed. He usually elected to stay put in the evening.

After he was sure everyone had gone for the night and the building had been dark for a while, Ian made his rounds, checking to be certain the doors were all locked. Sometimes he took a shower in the large bath off Plaid Lady's office, turning on the light in the tiled room only after he had shut the door, cleaning up carefully when he finished. In the chambers' storeroom, a coffeemaker always held some remaining coffee; there was sugar and

creamer on the table and, often, leftover doughnuts or cookies. With so many folks treating themselves, Ian felt his treat would not be noticed.

Every day other changes took place. The district
courtroom next to Plaid Lady's office was being
turned into a Christmas shop. Hordes of people,
"volunteers," Plaid Lady called them, showed up
each day to assemble fake Christmas trees and put
up shelving. Ian saw them come and go, nicely
dressed ladies, artists, and craftspeople hauling
boxes. Glass counters, called vitrines by the volunteers, were dollied in. Jean ran errands and went
out to get lunch for everyone.

Once in a while, Ian tracked Jean as she continued her investigation of the building. She had told
Plaid Lady that she wanted to find the holding cells
where criminals used to await trial. But with all the
high activity, she no longer wandered about as
much as before. Ian wondered if she was happier
now.

He hadn't seen her face since that first time. He
had watched her unload things at the main
entrance from a car he assumed was Plaid Lady's or
the Lady Leader's. She carried in armloads of
glossy posters, a bolt of silver cloth. He was careful
to stay back from the glass, but she never lifted her
face to his window again. Several times, she had
friends with her. They all wore the same oversize,

loose clothing Jean did, wrinkled looking, some even torn, as if they had gotten their clothes from Delbert Joe. It was difficult to distinguish some of the girls from the boys. He heard Jean address them as "dudes." They hauled in plywood, threaded pipe, and spools of wire. They carried labeled boxes of sound system speakers and theatrical lights.

At night, after everyone had left and Ian had checked the doors, he would explore to see what the day's activity had wrought. Movie Star Guy John David had thoroughly established his studio in the large room with the marble floor. Here he had made a marquee of some sort; Ian figured it would go over the entrance and cover the Hall of Justice letters. It was very lightweight for all its great size. Ian could lift it. It had little lightbulbs all around the periphery. At its center was a red sphere with the silver ARTlift logo slashed across it. The designer had also nailed and glued together from thick plywood a tall desk with a curving top and a trim high stool. Where would it go, Ian wondered.

He had noticed that everyone had been calling the circuit courtroom "the gallery." When he visited this gallery one evening, he saw that against one wall John David had taped up sketches of his "icon." Four upended benches rose like a great column from a penciled-in floor; on the very top sat a giant red sphere. *ARTlift* was written like a silver ribbon across its face. In the drawings, the icon looked as though it nearly reached the ceiling. How they were going to get that red ball on the top, Ian couldn't imagine. The ceiling was almost two stories high. John David's ladder, which lay on the floor by a side wall, didn't look as though it would be stable enough.

Then, early one morning, Ian heard Jean trill, "The cherry picker's here!" He hurried to the Assistant Prosecutor's office.

The "cherry picker" turned out to be a large hydraulic lift, delivered by an even larger forklift vehicle. Ian watched in awe from the windows over the main entrance. Movie Star Guy and Spy Hat had to take off a lot of doors to get the cherry picker lift inside. He heard the hammering and yelling and watched them carry the doors outside to the landing.

He climbed to the roof hut just in time to hear Jean cry out, "Whoop! Wheee-hooo!" The way her sound invaded the hut, Ian pictured her head just inches from the ceiling. She must be trying out the cherry picker. That was how the designer would get his sphere on top of the column of benches.

That night Ian visited Movie Star Guy's studio. How tidy the man was. He must clean up immediately after he finished a job. But more than that, things were attractively arranged, even brushes and hammers and cans of paint, which he had put on shelves like objects of art. His desk, one he had hammered together out of scraps, held a beautiful vase at one end and a sketch pad carefully opened to drawings of the gallery from various angles. Everything waited invitingly for the designer's return.

It made Ian remember hearing Jean discuss John David.

"I think he really loves harmony," Jean told her mother. "I think he'd probably die if he couldn't create wonderful things."

I guess, Ian thought, there are people who just want to make something for others to enjoy. Like the stories invented for Bams. He wondered if he could still do that, if he still had the gift of gab.

CHAPTER EIGHT

The Gnome

With so much happening each day, the old Hall of Justice changing under him, Ian was surprised one morning when no one arrived early to do anything. Sunday was when the church bells rang all over town, so he knew it wasn't Sunday now. Perhaps it was Saturday. The last time it was Saturday, though, there had been a lot of activity beneath him. Plaid Lady had bustled about; Movie Star Guy and Spy Hat had measured and talked and looked at the rolled-up papers. It could be Saturday now. Perhaps work at the Hall of Justice had finally settled into regular weekday hours.

Last night he had investigated the district courtroom by Plaid Lady's office. It had been transformed into a Christmas tree–filled gift store. A sign over the door said *HollyShop*.

Beautiful jewelry and holiday ornaments decorated the trees. Shelves were laden with bowls and
platters made of wood and glass and brightly
glazed clay; baskets of all sizes sat in groups on the
floor, some draped with soft woven shawls. Shirts
and dresses with odd designs painted on the front
and back, hats, and scarves were arranged against
a cloth-covered wall.

He had picked up a finely stitched notebook
that held paper so beautiful that Ian wouldn't have
wanted to write on it. There were several others;
they were all expensive—costing what ten restaurant meals or three weeks of groceries would have
been for Ian. He held them carefully, fascinated by
how much time and skill must have gone into making them—just so someone could look at them,
and hold them, and marvel.

There were paintings and statues and dolls,
wooden toys, and a dozen versions of Santa Claus;
one of them, wearing fringed leggings, sat in a
canoe with a raccoon perched in the bow. The
artists' names were on cards next to all the items.
Ian hadn't been able to tear himself away from
HollyShop. He had been very careful with what he
handled. He wound up a small carousel with
wooden horses and watched it whirl and blur,
unwinding. Would it belong in some small child's
room? He had tried to imagine the people whom

these gifts would surprise Christmas morning.

He and his father didn't celebrate Christmas. But usually, several days later, Ian would receive a present from his dad. Once it was a Swiss army knife, once a dark turtleneck. One time they went to a rink to skate. In return, Ian would listen especially well when his dad explained something to him. There was never anything else he could give his father.

On this Saturday he waited until he was sure there was no one else in the building. Then he went quietly down to the main floor to check out the results of yesterday's noisy activity—doors coming off, a huge machine delivering the cherry picker, Jean's excited hollering.

He found the cherry picker parked just outside the circuit courtroom. It dwarfed the hallway, a great steel box on wheels, painted yellow. It rested on a layer of hinged yellow rods. Ian examined it closely, guessing the rods would expand like an accordion to lift passengers in the box skyward. Beside the double doors of the circuit courtroom sat the high, curved desk, now painted red and black, trimmed in silver, out of which poked, at one end, a black lamp. Behind the desk was a tall red stool. Who will sit here, he wondered, and what for?

He didn't find a satisfactory answer in the courtroom itself. Rising up from the center of the great room were four benches standing on end, clamped solidly together. A swath of silvery fabric wound about the structure like an angel's scarf flowing from the top to the floor. In the pale light of morning sifting through the high windows, the new red carpet looked velvety and deep. The judge's bench had been transformed by vases holding black branches with red berries. The courtroom no longer looked like a courtroom. It looked as if it were waiting for something magnificent to happen.

A short while later, Plaid Lady and the Lady Leader surprised Ian when he heard their voices in the hall. He needn't have bothered hiding behind the jury room curtains. They only stayed for a half hour or so, first standing in the courtroom, which they kept calling the gallery, and then moving down the main hallway. When they left, the building seemed even more empty.

Because there was no activity for him to keep track of and because he no longer worried about finding food, the mystery of his father's disappearance began to torment him. He was certain that his father had seen all the comings and goings in and around the Hall of Justice and was staying away. That was it. He tried to figure out a way to signal his father that he was still here. He checked the basement storage bin and found his father's coat and his own note just as he had left them. He crossed out *October* and wrote in *November.*

He knew that any writing on the outside of the building or on windows would be wiped off and would send signals to others besides his father.

"I'm here," he said aloud to the empty air as he wandered through the building. "Dad, I'm still here."

Outside it had begun to rain, a cold November rain. The navy coat was probably waterproof. Perhaps he would go out later. A worry about encountering Birthday Boy on a Saturday made him put that excursion off. Although he had taken the precaution of removing the label from the navy coat and inking his name there instead, using scissors and a felt-tip pen from Plaid Lady's office, he couldn't relax in its warmth.

Filled with loneliness and worry, he began to eat although he wasn't hungry. He had shopped for food supplies yesterday and stored them carefully. But his father's training was disintegrating. His dad always selected graham crackers over chocolate chip cookies, whole wheat raisin bread over soft white, skim milk because it lasted longer. Cheese lasted longer than bologna. Oranges kept; bananas did not. Peanut butter kept; butter did not.

Ian had begun to ease in a few forbidden items. He loved bananas and chocolate chip cookies. On this weekend, he devoured four pounds of bananas, two large boxes of Famous Amos chocolate chip cookies, and most of the other foodstuffs he'd brought in, including the peanut butter and raisin bread. The half gallon of 2 percent chocolate milk he drank all in one sitting. Then he felt awful— bloated and log-headed. And guilty. He was letting things go to pieces. His father would not approve.

The rain turned into snow, and Ian went out for a walk as the early dark came. He needed to clear his head and energize his leaden body. He would get hold of himself. He would figure out a code for his father. He would monitor his own behavior. The snow fell gently, softening his despair. When he returned, it felt good to get back into his building. He slept fitfully under his coat, and in the morning it was twisted around him.

On Sunday, it seemed even quieter. Outside it was still snowing. Sobered by the bad food experience of the day before, Ian took some more paper from Plaid Lady's ample supply and wrote down a list of what foods he would buy later on. Bananas and chocolate chip cookies were not on this list— nor chocolate milk. He couldn't even bear to think of them. Next he listed what he would eat and what time he would do this. Then he counted his money. He still had thirty-four dollars and some change.

"What next, Dad?" he asked the wall. What would his dad have done when *he* was eleven?

Ian tried to imagine his father as a boy. He wouldn't have had a beard or a long ponytail tied with a leather thong. Ian had seen pictures of his dad as a kid with his dad's older sister. They were standing astride their bikes and squinting at the sun. His dad's hair had been very red back then, short and red. Now only his beard had red in it. Ian's grandmother had taken the picture. Her shadow lay across the grass in front of her two children. His grandmother had been dead now for three years. He remembered her hair, pale reddish and thin; her hands were long with knobby fingers. She had smelled of housework—Fels Naptha soap and Clorox—and gravy; she had smelled of gravy, too. Ian controlled the sudden desire to eat.

His grandmother had had a strong voice, his father said. "Mitchell," she had called the little boy who was his father. "Mitchell, stop chasing the chickens." His father had told him that once.

Ian remembered her voice, too. "I couldn't get your father to leave those birds alone," she told Ian in that far time when he was a little boy. His grandmother had missed her chickens. The farm wasn't much of a farm anymore, she told him. No cows. No real crop. Just a kitchen garden and an old orchard. "Your father could make it pay if he'd get off his duff," said his grandmother, and added wistfully, "But he don't have the heart for it."

Ian shook himself, scattering memories. He decided to make a careful round of the building, select a good bathroom, and experiment with his hair disguise game.

Movie Star Guy's big, graceful room with the marble floor drew him. It was warm there. The tall windows framed the snow falling through gray light. Ian walked around the space, admiring. Movie Star Guy's desk had a pretty pattern of paint spatters on it. In the center, the sketchbook sat at what seemed a perfect angle. Bare branches were arranged like flowers in the large vase. There was a big, airy bathroom right next door. Ian decided not to use this one for his hair games.

"I'm being careful, Dad," he said as he left the graceful room. He took the elevator, just for the noise that enlivened the quiet. The bathrooms on the second floor were all rusty and bad smelling. Ian took the elevator back to the main floor. It would be much more pleasant to do the hair game in a clean place. He chose one of the jury bathrooms behind the courtroom they were now calling the gallery.

Ian took off his coat and folded it carefully on one of the several chairs. He soaped his hair into a point that lopped over sort of like the meringue on a lemon pie. It was getting too long to stand straight up. His father, who carried barber scissors snapped in a narrow case inside his backpack, always gave Ian his haircuts. Ian was just plastering two serpentine curls around his ears when he heard a distant door slam. He froze, hands filled with soap.

The weekend silence was all that greeted his alert ears and a few soft pops of soap bubbles. But he was sure he had heard a door. He dared not run water or pull out a paper towel. Using his thumb and one finger, he turned the knob and opened the door a crack. Silence.

Cautiously Ian stepped out into the hallway. Soapy water was running down the back of his neck. He strained to listen through the soap fizzing in his ears. Silence hovered.

Slowly, close to the wall, Ian crept down to the south corridor and paused at the corner. He kept his breathing shallow. Listened. Silence sang.

He had just turned to go back to the clean bathroom when the air around him suddenly burst, full of movement, the brush of a live body, a splitting yell.

"Whooo . . . ooh-whoa!!" A sharp, fresh smell. Little half-glasses perched in curly hair—tall, very tall shape. The odor of mint and lemons and wet snow.

Ian stared for one moment only. Movie Star Guy's blue, blue eyes were widened in disbelief. Neither waited past that instant. Movie Star Guy turned and sprinted away. Ian ran back, grabbed his coat from the bathroom, then hurried silently through the circuit courtroom to the north stairs. He would rinse off in one of the second-floor bathrooms. Then he'd leave the building. Movie Star Guy would call the police. He was probably in Plaid Lady's office doing that right now.

His father had said that the safest place from danger was usually the closest to it—so you could study it. Ian decided to get as close as he could to Plaid Lady's office. First rinse off on the second floor.

He was careless with the paper towels, using as many as he needed to get his hair as dry as possible, stuffing them wet into the wall container.

He was standing at his stairway post when the police arrived and he heard Movie Star Guy's breathless explanation.

"I hardly believe what I'm saying. This . . . this *creature* . . . some sort of gnome or elf. But tall. Its hair! It came to a pointy curl thing—like frosting."

The two policemen looked at each other. One of them ran his hand over his face and Ian got the feeling he was smiling behind the hand.

"I am *not* a lunatic," protested Movie Star Guy.

"Well," said the smiler. "It don't sound like Delbert Joe."

"Who," inquired Movie Star Guy in an outraged voice, "is Delbert Joe?"

"He belongs to the blue blanket outside," said the other cop. "But I don't think he could get inside."

"This creature was thin, sort of crouching—like a gnome. He had this strange hair—white hair. I am not given to fantasy," protested Movie Star Guy.

"We'll call it in. They'll come, check out the whole building," said the smiler.

That was what Ian needed to hear. He'd remove all traces. Any food that was left, his backpack. He'd check all the rooms he used, and then he'd leave and come back late tonight. He felt his father's spirit in him, chasing loneliness. He would not leave a crumb or a footprint.

But it was well after dark, after he'd returned and had begun to settle himself down to sleep, when the police sweep began. He heard them on the first floor. At the same time, others thumped up the stairs. Ian leaped to his feet, grabbing his coat and backpack and hurried down the hallway to the dark Fifth District County courtroom centered on his floor, the one he normally hurried past. He had just slipped inside when he heard the noisy banging of doors at the end of the hall. In the darkness, he groped around. The air was dusty and dry. *To be safest from danger, get closer to it.* Ian flattened himself right by the door trying to breathe easily as his father had taught him.

He heard voices outside and the faint squeal of the door opening. It swung inward, sandwiching Ian, hiding him against the wall. A flashlight beam danced and swung around the courtroom. It was the first time Ian had seen what the place looked like. The beam swept along the judge's bench, the spectator seats, and into corners like a missile tracking body heat.

"No gnomes here," joked the voice in the doorway to someone down the hall. Their laughter and the flashlight beam were both eclipsed, sliced by the closing door. The darkness was made darker by the sudden absence of light.

It was only then Ian became aware of another presence in the room. A shuddering escape of breath. Did he imagine it? Was the darkness all at once warmer?

It took all of his willpower, all his father's training, to keep Ian from bolting out of the room and into the uniformed arms of the police.

CHAPTER NINE

The Arrival

Ian stood in darkness, stomach tight with fear. The police sweep, which normally took twenty minutes or so, seemed to go on forever. Holding his breath still, he waited for another sign that someone else was in the room. At the same time, he kept his ears tuned for the end of the search. In his anxiety, could his mind have played tricks on him? Had he really heard another's breathing? Just as he marked the sound of the police leaving below, a hoarse jabbering began in the darkness around him.

"Fool boy, fool boy, fool boy . . ."

Over and over like a chant—now close, now farther away, it beat against the darkness.

"Fool boy, fool boy . . ." The jabbering rose into the air, *became* the air, and then there was this sour smell, swampy and stale—old cigarettes and urine.

The chanting stopped suddenly. Ian felt movement where the chant had been. Then, clear and
loud, a voice said, "The law is an ass."

The voice released Ian. Gripping his possessions, he leaped to the door and tore from the
room. Behind him he heard, "Fool boy. Fool boy."
Then strange, loose laughter as though something
were being shaken from the speaker's body.

He barred himself into the room for miniature
people. Listened, crouching at the door for a long
time before he thought he detected shuffling footsteps heading to the stairway. Toward morning he
dropped off to sleep, his head against the door.

He slept several hours later than usual and was
awakened by Jean's distant voice shouting from
outside the building. He unbarred his door to find
an empty hallway—no jabbering man—and he
hurried to the Assistant Prosecutor's office.

He entered the room cautiously, eyes searching.
It appeared empty. Bright sunlight lay in warm
shafts across the bare floor and a few scattered
chairs, dissolving most of his remaining fear. He
went to the window.

Again Jean's voice rang from outside. Maybe she
had been waiting to let someone in. Ian couldn't
see her but could hear her hollering at the hidden
concourse door.

"Sam! John David! Mr. Case! They're here! Somebody get Sam! They're here! The kites are here!"

Suddenly she appeared below and bounded, coat flying, down the wide steps to the bottom, where a big rig was slowly backing right up over the curb to the wheelchair ramp. Jean began to guide the driver, using her arms.

Most of the snow had melted away. The day was bright, the streets drying. Ian noticed Delbert Joe's blue blanket in a rumpled heap at the foot of the wide steps. This was definitely the best spot to view the activity outside.

Ian watched the tricky inch-by-inch progress of the van as it eased up to the ramp. Plaid Lady came striding out, bellowing, "Tallyho!" followed by Movie Star Guy and Spy Hat.

The driver jumped down from his cab and climbed up at the rear of the trailer to open the heavy barred doors whose bottom half lowered into a ramp. Ian peered curiously into the gray interior but could only make out a load of crates. He was growing hungry, but he watched as the driver pulled a dolly from the interior and began to hoist crates against its heavy back and wheel them down the ramp. He left them on the sidewalk and climbed back to get more.

Plaid Lady examined each crate where it stood, marking something on the clipboard she carried. She had the truck driver turn the crates so she could check all sides. The truck driver began to wear a cross expression.

Plaid Lady ignored him, continuing, with the same care, to look over each crate as it was unloaded. It took a long time to check them all. She strode around poking at the wood, clutching the clipboard. A couple of crates seemed to be slightly damaged. Plaid Lady marked them down. Finally, she handed the clipboard to the driver. He signed it with an exasperated shake of his head, gave it back, then heaved himself into his cab.

All the goings-on outside had chased away the last of Ian's fear. His head, groggy from his uncomfortable sleep, began to clear.

Movie Star Guy was strong. He loaded crates onto the dolly—huge things, some of them, towering way over his head. The man's face beneath his curly crop of hair was determined, the set of his back and shoulders urgent as he rolled crate after crate up the ramp along the side of the building. Here Ian lost sight of him but knew he must be coming in the back door behind the circuit courtroom. They would be using the wooden wedge to peg the door open. Movie Star Guy was fast, too. Ian had assumed that a guy so handsome and deliberate in his dress, a guy who had run away from him, was probably kind of wimpy. Wrong.

Spy Hat, Jean, and Plaid Lady helped each other load crates on another dolly. They took longer than Movie Star Guy, who moved as though he had a plan in mind that might disappear if he didn't hurry. Jean, after helping load only three crates onto the dolly, had to take off her jacket and drape it over the stair railing.

Some of the crates looked like they might have bodies in them. Ian remembered hearing something about kites going up in the great circuit courtroom, but it must be something else was going to be put there. Maybe statues. Kites were bright, flimsy triangles made of paper with string tails. They were hard to get up into the air and, when you did, they got caught in trees all the time. His grandmother had been very good at getting kites into the air. And getting Ian's out of the apple trees.

Below, Jean was trying to carry two tubes twice as long as she was up the main steps. One wing of her almost-black hair was tucked behind her ear, the other fell across her cheek. Halfway up to the first landing, one of the tubes slipped from under her arm and began to roll, thumpety-thump, back down the steps. Ian could hear her high, clear laugh, peal after peal, accompanying the thumps of the tube. He found himself smiling, a funny feeling on his face. He watched her struggle up the remaining steps, where he lost sight of her but could hear more muffled laughter as she tried to get in one of the doors. How different her delighted laugh was from the low, serious voice he had often heard.

When the last crate had left the sidewalk in front of the building, Ian pondered over where he could next follow the action below.

He climbed to the roof hut and stood on the steel walkway, straining his ears. He could hear faint voices and muffled thumps. Once a cry that must have been Jean. They had very likely taken the crates into the large room marked JURY or some of the smaller rooms behind the courtroom.

"This place is bathroom city!" It was Jean's voice. She had come into the courtroom below. "Nearly every office back there has its own. They're all rusty and yucky looking. Sam says they might not all flush. She's saving money by only having toilets cleaned that will be used by the public and our staff and the volunteers. The kite insurance alone," she confided to the designer, "is over $100,000. Mom has been complaining all week about that little expense."

"I see groups—no, *schools* of kites—like *fish* swimming in the atmosphere . . ." It was Movie Star Guy in another part of the gallery, his excited tumble of words rising to where Ian stood.

"Can we open the crates now?" asked Jean. "I'm dying to see the shark one—and there's this ninety-five-foot Chinese dragon. He—or rather, *she* would be great all by herself." Her low voice was thoughtful. "Who says a dragon has to be a he-dragon? I think the dragon is a she-dragon."

"Like mother, like daughter," sang out Movie Star Guy. A door slammed. The voices became faint.

When Ian next looked out the window over the main entrance, Jean's jacket was still hanging over the railing. His insides gave a lurch, torn between the leftover desire for a coat and something else. He was surprised to discover a wealth of friendly, protective feelings for this girl with almost-black hair who sometimes seemed so unhappy but whose high, clean laugh could burst from her with such delight.

⋅⇥◉⇤⋅

MUSEUM TO SPONSOR KITE SHOW, *said the headline. Patient 227 read the paper now every day— every word. Even the ads. Even the obituaries. The lost and found. He filled his head with words from the newspaper, and he could keep the words there filling up blank spaces like a moving neon message across a marquee.*

An exciting addition to the holiday festivities in downtown Grand River opens with ARTlift, an exhibition of more than two hundred kites.

Kites. Patient 227 remembered kites. As a boy, he'd been good with them, could get them higher than the apple trees. Flew them out in the field in April winds. There had been one kite with a spider on it he especially loved—a wicked kite, pale blue with a black tarantula spread across. When you got it up and flying, the pale blue blended with sky and it seemed the huge spider was crawling across the heavens. The memory did not hurt. Where had that been?

You won't recognize the former Hall of Justice at the corner of Division and Michigan Streets. The greater part of the first floor in this grand old building will house not only the kite exhibition, but a Christmas gift boutique filled with hand-crafted treasures by area artists, and an activities area, KIDlift, where young folks can make their own kites, write poetry, invent games, and design a kite to hang on the wishing tree.

The words filed into Patient 227's head and suddenly stopped. He stared at the paragraph. He read the first lines several times, trying to quiet the quick and terrible thumping of his heart. Former Hall of Justice. Former Hall of Justice. Grand old building. *These words would not march obediently into his mind.*

He let the paper fall, rustling to the floor—loud, too loud, the sound of paper like fire crackling through weeds. In his ears spun a high whine, drowning out the noise of the paper, of a heart thumping. His head was shrinking. It became a heavy ball—a bowling ball, a golf ball, a rabbit dropping. Something like sleep came. He sank gratefully into its embrace.

CHAPTER TEN

THE KITES

Movie Star Guy and Spy Hat were staying late in the building again. Ian could hear their voices and an occasional thump in the rooms behind the courtroom gallery. Their presence kept away fear, so he decided to make the rounds of all the rooms on the second floor while they were still below. He crept carefully down to Plaid Lady's office and borrowed the flashlight from her storeroom.

Armed with light, he returned to the second floor and checked offices and bathrooms, utility closets and the north courtroom. He investigated the dark, ominous Fifth District County courtroom. Propping the door open so he would have a little extra light, he walked boldly into the gloom. *Never act like a victim.* He shone the flashlight into every nook and corner, behind the judge's bench, in the jury box, the witness stand. The light switch he found required a special key. Before he left, he remembered to look behind the door. The room was empty. The jabbering man was not on the second floor. Nor was he on the roof.

Ian slipped down the stairs to the basement. He turned on the lights in each empty office. He investigated the toilets and the storage stacks. In the bin where his father had put his coat, Ian found the note still there. He looked in the boiler room with its booming furnace, opened the refrigerator because he couldn't resist the impulse. It was bare as a bone. Satisfied that the jabbering man was not in the basement, he returned to his stairway post.

As Spy Hat and Movie Star Guy were leaving, Ian heard them talking about getting dinner downtown and then returning.

"Eleven more crates to open," said Spy Hat. "Piece o' cake with that power screwdriver."

"Can you imagine how long it would have taken fifty years ago?" Movie Star Guy laughed, patting his tool belt. "BT? Before Technology?"

When they were gone, Ian left his post and made certain all exit doors were closed. Then he checked the first floor before returning the flashlight.

Satisfied the building was empty, he decided to have dinner downtown, too. It was tempting to immediately visit the rooms behind the courtroom where the crates were, but he was hungry. He was also tired of peanut butter and raisin bread. A warm meal would be good. He could check out the crates later tonight. But first, he would leave a series of little traps to signal him, when he returned, if the jabbering man had gotten back in.

He left a folded piece of paper tucked in each of the outside doors that would fall out if the door was opened. As a last caution, he left the water running a little in the sink of the men's room. His father's trick. "No one can resist turning off running water," his father said. "It's a built-in instinct." If the faucet was turned off when he came back, someone would have been there.

The two men were coming back later; they would use either one of the main doors or the side door near the crates. Ian would try to get back before they came.

Feeling secure, Ian put on Birthday Boy's coat and walked downtown.

But he felt noticeable as a neon sign in the navy coat when he entered the Coffee Plantation. His quick appraisal shot a warning. At the back of the restaurant, deep in conversation, sat Movie Star Guy and Spy Hat. Ian controlled the instinct to turn and run. *Cool it. Act natural. They don't know you.* Birthday Boy, whom he expected to see at every turn, did not appear and claim his coat. In fact, no one paid him any particular attention. So Ian relaxed at one of the little tables and ordered a hot corned beef sandwich, a cup of cappuccino, and pumpkin pie.

"Anyone with you, honey?" asked the pleasant waitress. "Your mama le'cha drink coffee?" Encouraged by her homely niceness, Ian said, "My mom lets me drink this kind. It has a lot of milk. We're going to a movie later." He began to feel comfortable in his daring, pretending his lie was true. At times like this, he thought he might still have, buried inside, the gift of gab.

After eating, Ian got up to go to the bathroom in the back of the restaurant mainly so he could see Movie Star Guy and Spy Hat up close. Perhaps they would glance at him, would see this normal-looking kid who was going to join his mother for a movie, would nod or smile. They looked different from this angle, their heads smaller. Spy Hat's hat was on a chair. He had dark hair and deep-set dark eyes. The pair was still deep in conversation and did not notice him as he slowly passed. Spy Hat was drawing with his pen on a napkin. Ian felt disappointment like a soft slap. Dumb. Why would I want them to look at me? he asked himself on his way back to the Hall of Justice, his father's voice in his head.

113

No one had entered while he'd been gone. The little wads of paper were still in place. He checked the men's room. No one had turned off the water. Ian shut the faucet.

Other people came to the building that evening. The Lady Leader made a visit. He heard her pleasant, low voice in the courtroom below: "Just get the lids off so we can have a peek . . ." and then her laugh, rich and controlled. But most of the activity was coming from the several rooms behind the courtroom. He could feel excitement pulsing up toward where he stood on the steel walkway of the little roof hut.

A host of voices passed through the courtroom below, eager and bright with pleasure. Another lovely laugh from the Lady Leader chimed upward. It reminded Ian of Jean's. Someone said, "Spectacular!" so clearly that Ian glanced nervously about his space. But they all appeared to be leaving. Soon he could visit the crates.

It was well past eleven, however, when everyone had finally left. Eleven in *real* time. The clocks, still on old daylight saving time, read midnight. Ian visited all the doors again. Only two in the bank of front doors had lost their paper scraps when the museum people left. He repositioned the folded paper in these doors, then checked all the others. The papers were in place everywhere.

Ian found that the lights in the rooms behind the circuit courtroom were still on. The building was high enough so that no one could see him from the street. Three offices behind the circuit courtroom were filled with crates—every room except the jury room. Some of the lids were up. Styrofoam packing material lay around in messy piles.

The first crate he looked into was filled with lumpy, wrapped bundles. He moved on. The second was as tall as he was and as long. It was marked U.S.A. Careful not to disturb the packing material, he peered inside. It was divided into long compartments by plywood. The first compartment held a fragile canoe, very old, small enough for a doll. Two gulls lay inside the canoe attached to long, thin dowels. The other compartments in this crate supported cardboard folders tied at the tops with ribbon. Ian went to a third crate marked CHINESE.

This crate was closed, smaller than the others. It came almost up to his chest. Ian lifted the lid and there, supported by bands beneath its frame, was the intricate body of a dragon with a ferocious head. Ian could see down into the well of the body. It was delicately made of thin, nearly transparent paper over a skeleton of slender curved rods. He half expected to find a dragon heart nestling in the cage of its chest. The paper was beautifully painted outside to represent scales and muscle. Three pairs of wings were held against the wall of the crate by Velcro bands. On the opposite wall of the crate were fastened two pairs of legs.

Ian couldn't resist. He wanted to see the splendid beast from the outside. He wanted to see it with its wings and legs attached. The dragon, like people, would be more interesting straight on than seen from overhead.

He closed his eyes. "I know you would say no, Dad," he said, his voice sounding hollow in the silence.

Carefully, Ian unhooked the bands supporting the paper-covered skeleton and lifted the dragon body from its foam bed. How light it was for something so beautiful and fierce. The red-lined mouth was open in a silent hiss. Two long eyeteeth descended from the sharp rows lining the open maw. "Oh," breathed Ian. "Oh, dragon. King of Dragons."

He checked the body to see where the legs attached; the little ones must go near the tail. Now he noticed that the midsized pair of wings would slide in above them. The great wings of blue and yellow had dowels that inserted at the shoulder; beneath went the large legs with their long talons. With all the gentleness he could muster, balancing the dragon body with one hand, Ian put him together, careful not to tangle the several strings. The strings at the shoulder and tail, Ian figured, must be how the dragon would be hung. From the ceiling. The heavier string was, maybe, for flying the dragon. He fastened the tiny flame-colored wings behind the head.

Then, both hands supporting it under the belly, he held the dragon at arm's length and looked at it. The colors on the outside were brilliant, the details of scale and tendon elegant.

When the distant door slammed, he froze, thinking guiltily it was his father. Then he realized someone was approaching careless of the noise. Not his father.

He couldn't stuff the dragon back into the crate, crushing its wings. He couldn't even put the dragon down without endangering its delicate legs with their tipped claws. There was no time to plan. With one hand, he closed the lid. Holding the dragon over his head, he eased out the door and through the back hallway, then down the south corridor, past the library and the holding cells.

"I knew we left the lights on." Movie Star Guy had returned with someone else.

Ian hurried on, the dragon held aloft, praying no one would look in the empty crate. He didn't need another encounter with this man.

"Careless, careless," he said aloud back in the

room for miniature people. So many mistakes. He was out of control again. Childish. Dumb things, things he thought he wanted, got in the way. Having fun got in the way. His father would not appreciate that. He fixed his chair bolt at the door with one hand while the other held the King of Dragons, his thoughtless mistake.

But the dragon was magical. Ian suspended him, hooking the top strings over one of the low, arched windows. When he lay down and turned his head toward the window, the splendid beast was silhouetted against the Christmas lights across the way. Then Ian slept. It was a deep sleep during which, this time, the dragon carried *him.*

He sat behind the great blue-and-yellow wings, hands resting lightly on the shoulders where the wings were joined. There were no dowel sticks. Instead of a cavity shaped of curved rods, there were powerful muscles and warmth beneath the iridescent scales.

Before him the great wings rose and fell. He could feel the pull and release of tendons under his hands. It was daylight saving time. Far below him was an endless sunny landscape filled with animals—deer and rabbit, bear and squirrel, horse and steer and tiger. The wings rose and fell, untiring.

Then, in a breath, he was the dragon, wings beating from his own shoulders. Fascinated by the creatures below, he was afraid to startle them with his strangeness if he came to the ground. So he flew on, growing tired. In the distance, there was another dragon, dark against the far sky. One like him, the only other dragon in this exotic but familiar world. Ian couldn't tell if it was flying in his direction or away, if it was friend or foe. Should he fly toward him? Should he call out? There was a name on his tongue.

Now he had to struggle to keep his wings working. They seemed so heavy. He made a great effort to hail the distant dragon—a fading shape—and awakened in the room for miniature people with his arms jerking. He was breathing hard, glad to be back—and, at the same time, sorry. He lay for a time with his eyes on the dragon shape silhouetted against the twinkle of red and green.

When morning spread its grayness across the window and dimmed the lights of Christmas, he took the beast down and, carrying him with great gentleness, returned to the room where he had found him. He hated to remove the wings and stood undecided in front of the crate a bit too long. The pale light began to brighten. Voices outside warned him away; there was no time to disassemble the dragon and return the parts to the crate. He looped the strings to the top corners of the door near the crate marked CHINESE and hurried through the back hallways to the second floor. *Careless. Careless. Too many mistakes.*

All day he observed what he could of the unpacking of the crates. He crouched on the steel grating above the circuit courtroom they were calling the gallery. He nibbled on graham crackers and raisins; they were easy to carry and gave off no telling odor. He listened, trying to identify an activity below from the sound it made. Most of the unpacking went on in the rooms and hallway behind the courtroom where the crates had been set. The shouts and thumps, doors closing, things being dragged, were muffled sounds. He couldn't isolate the action, but there was a high excitement about it—like indoor recess on a rainy day. Ian was warmed by his fascination. Jean, he discovered, was bored.

"This should be exciting as Christmas," he heard her complain when she came into the gallery directly beneath. "But it's boring, boring. I mean—they're taking a picture of *everything* back there—the crate before it's unpacked, the empty crate, the packing around the kite when it's removed, then the kite itself, then close-ups of any damage. I mean, how do you photograph mildew or a bad smell? Come on. They're logging in a notebook every broken dowel and every teeny rip. And they're checking numbers against lists and making new numbers for the photographs. It's deadly. It's killing all the fun."

Then Ian learned that Jean was also angry.

"Plus, I keep getting blamed for assembling that beautiful dragon before they had time to photograph the packing and all. My mom says that it's just like me not to think before I act."

Ian felt a wave of guilt sweep over him. How could he undo his error? His father always said, "Don't backtrack to follow a mistake." Ian shook away the bad feeling, knowing he must let this mistake work itself out. *Learn and move on.*

But despite all the tedious, methodical care unpacking the crates, Jean did get excited.

"Oh, John David, look at this!"

Ian felt her joy with relief. Something was, for the moment, lifting this girl from her restless displeasure.

"It's a phoenix! Its head is like a flame! An enormous flame!"

Movie Star Guy seemed just as overjoyed and raved about some details in the feathers.

"They're still photographing the body and the tail. And the wings. The wings are enormous!"

"Jean!"

It was the Lady Leader, Jean's mother, from somewhere behind the gallery, sounding slightly muffled and slightly miffed. "We need that head back here. We're not through with it."

Then she came into the gallery below, her voice crisp and commanding.

"This stuff has to be packed up again in nine weeks. And packed RIGHT. We can make that job easier NOW. You'll be glad of all our care in unpacking when you're staring at a Japanese fighter trying to figure out whether it gets tied in an acid-free folder or wrapped in treated tissue and placed in a box."

"Couldn't we just invent that part when the time comes?" asked Jean. "It seems like an awful waste of time."

"This collection is worth a fortune, Jean. A fortune!" The Lady Leader was upset. "It has to be packed exactly right or the insurance isn't worth a hoot if there's some kind of accident."

There was a long, heavy silence. The Lady Leader broke it. "Let me remind you, young lady, that this is a job, not a party."

Ian heard, or imagined he heard, a strong sigh. Jean? Her mother?

Then Ian thought they must have gone back to the crates. It was silent below for a long time except for the stirrings of, probably, Movie Star Guy. Ian dozed off and on.

At lunchtime, Ian overheard another conversation. Over the rustle of paper bags below, voices rose with the lovely smell of hamburgers and French fries to where Ian sat chewing raisins.

"I checked the storeroom and the crafts inventory and had the volunteers look for anything missing. Everything seems to be where it's supposed to be," said Plaid Lady.

"Why wouldn't it?" Jean's mother asked.

"John David saw someone strange in the back hallway on Sunday," Jean said with hushed excitement.

"I knew it!" Plaid Lady bragged. "I knew all along someone was hiding in the building."

"Who was hiding?" The Lady Leader sounded grim. "What did he look like, John David?"

The designer didn't answer right away. Ian listened. He could feel a smile softening his own face.

"The police didn't find anyone when they searched. I don't think they believed me."

This time, Jean asked. "So—what did he look like? Do you think the blue blanket is his?"

"Some kind of . . . of night person, an underground person—like a gnome."

Ian suppressed a snicker.

"Like a . . . a fish you might find down five miles deep. No eyes. No color."

"He had no eyes?!" gasped Jean with delighted horror. Ian stifled a gasp of his own.

"No. Yes. I mean he had eyes. That was figurative. He was just . . . unearthly . . . unholy . . . unimaginable."

Ian grabbed his mouth with both hands, rocking back and forth on the steel grating, controlling an explosion of laughter.

"Hush," warned the Lady Leader. "We don't want to frighten away our volunteers back there."

"Or," said Plaid Lady, "distract those students from MSU's art department. There're still seventeen crates and those four tubes to log in."

There were a lot of groans. It seemed that Jean wasn't the only bored one.

⋅→⇒◉⇐←⋅

Patient 227 sat in the solarium where recovering patients were allowed. There were hanging plants and a comfortable moistness warmed by the sun through slanted windows. It was a room designed to make you feel good, but Patient 227 didn't notice because he had been busy counting. Counting years. Backtracking.

1950. Fell down the front steps, stared forever at the underside of the porch roof. Mother's hands, rough and gentle. Her lap, the hooknosed doctor with the needle. And screaming.

Patient 227 figured back from his first day of school—then figured forward to the date on the newspaper he held in his hand. It took all morning for him to know he was fifty years old. Half a century. There were some heavy blank spots somewhere past high school. He remembered a pretty girl, a cheerleader he'd stolen from Hardy, the forward on his team. There had been a locker room fight. Cut his lip, banged Hardy up bad. Felt worse afterward. Couldn't remember her name now. She wore his basketball letter like a beacon, prancing with her books down the school hallways. Pretty girl.

He didn't feel fifty. He didn't feel tired at all—or old as fifty had seemed to him at sixteen. He kept looking at his hands. Looking. They seemed so wise. If he could ask his hands . . .

It wasn't until the next day that he remembered, briefly, he had a son.

"We weren't going to have any kids . . . ever," he said aloud, accusingly, to no one—to her? Then the memory slipped away like smoke.

CHAPTER ELEVEN

Freedom and Comfort

People came and went all day and on into the evening. Volunteers were replaced by more volunteers. They were all ages and sizes. Ian watched them from his window post overlooking the main entrance. Hairdo'ed ladies wearing suits and carrying purses, women and men in jeans and parkas, and, later, folks in business clothes and teenagers in their bulky, dragging pants—everybody came to help unpack the kites. It was late when the building was empty.

Ian took his time checking rooms and testing doors to make certain they were secure. The basement offices and furnace room now had an ominous tomblike feel to them—as if *things* were lurking in every shadow. These rooms he always checked while Spy Hat and Movie Star Guy were still working in the gallery. He felt safer that way. Today there had been many people staying late, but Ian had risked discovery to sneak down the north stairs to the basement rather than deal with these rooms when the building rang with emptiness. He was pretty sure no volunteer would descend into the unfriendly dark offices below the street level, but he had taken extra care to be noiseless as he made his rounds.

After everyone had left, he borrowed Plaid Lady's flashlight again and made the second-floor rounds, whirling about, every so often, to look behind when he imagined footsteps. Satisfied at last that the second-floor offices and courtrooms housed no jabbering man, he took the elevator to the main floor. He had saved the best for last.

Checking the main floor was a pleasure. He could now see, firsthand, the progress he had only partially grasped from above. There was nothing fearful about the main floor with its newly bright hallways and carpeting, and the aura of expectation that hovered about all the preparations. No one lurked in the clean corners; the shadows hid nothing.

In the courtroom gallery, the first thing Ian saw was the cherry picker near the center of the room. Directly above, suspended like a guardian over all, hung the King of Dragons. It was the only kite up.

The rest had been placed all about the room, waiting to be assembled. Owls and turtles lay by a sign marked THAILAND. Cobras and snakes with fabulous tails were draped over the few remaining benches. Tigers and more tigers were spread on the floor with a placard that read JAPAN. Leaning against one wall were a host of clean-cut, flat blue-and-red kites tagged TAGASAKI FIGHTERS. There were fighter kites from Korea, too. Chinese kites with gorgeously painted scenes lay on the judge's bench along with huge beetles and bugs and butterflies. A crumpled heap of black cloth wore a sign that read SHARK, AMERICAN. Piled by one wall was the head of a Chinese tiger on top of a stack of striped disks. The striped part is probably the body, thought Ian, wondering how it would fly. All these kites were supposed to fly, he'd overheard. There were other American kites, Australian kites, Portuguese kites, Canadian kites, and kites called deltas, a box kite from England. There were kites made of silk, of rice paper, of newspaper, and postage stamps. There were gigantic kites and kites no larger than a thumbnail.

In the offices behind the courtroom gallery, Ian examined notebooks lying open on crates, looked at listings. Picked up one of three cameras sitting on the floor. Thirty-one shots had been taken.

Later that night, when he lay down to sleep in

the room for miniature people, the marvels below him seemed to cast a safe spell over the Hall of Justice. He got up from the floor, anyway, and barred the door as usual.

In the morning, he hurried from post to post in his eagerness to see what would happen next below him.

Once, in the roof hut, he heard a conversation that made him more wary than ever.

"Little things," Plaid Lady was saying, "make me uneasy. I get here in the morning before anyone else and I get this sense of being watched." She snorted. "And then there was the mystery of those small crumpled bits of paper—like 'hello'—whenever I came in the front door—even after I knew I'd picked them up the day before. I don't find them anymore, but . . ."

"It would unnerve me, too." The voice was Jean's. ". . . all alone in this ancient old place. I'd feel watched."

"You can have another doughnut," said Plaid Lady. Then Jean's voice dropped so low he could barely hear her.

"Do you believe in ghosts?"

"Yeah, right," said Plaid Lady. "Thanks a lot, Jean."

"No, really. I mean," said Jean, enthusiasm surging in her, "like before you moved all your stuff into your office, didn't it just reek of someone else who'd spent a lot of time here—like lived a part of their life here?"

There was a pause before Plaid Lady answered. "In a way, yes," she finally admitted. "Of course, I don't feel edgy or secretly observed when someone else is here." She gave her snort of a laugh. "Even a lame-butt teenager who seeks out diversions like ghosts."

"I'm actually serious," said Jean. "I mean, it could explain a lot of things. Like with the smaller Chinese dragon, the lovely one with three pairs of wings. My mom thinks I just had to put it together."

Ian winced, then listened carefully to see where his mistake would go.

"Oh?" asked Plaid Lady.

"Couldn't it have been some sort of ghost?"

"Jean. Where are you going with this?" asked Plaid Lady. But she didn't wait for an answer. She interrupted herself. "I'm sure there's a very reasonable explanation."

Plaid Lady doesn't believe Jean, thought Ian. Relief and guilt mingled uncomfortably in him.

"I think this wonderful old building is loaded with the remnants of lives already lived," continued Plaid Lady. "It's casting a spell of anxiety over the entire staff. Even your mom, and nothing ever shakes her up. We mustn't let it get to the volunteers. We need every one of them."

But the volunteers kept coming. Some arrived to replace the morning ones who were leaving. Ian could hear John David's instructions as they began to assemble kites in the gallery.

Later, by the side door, Jean speculated to Plaid Lady as they pulled on their coats to leave the building.

"I wonder if the ghost owner of the blue blanket has moved. Maybe he's found a better place. When I came in his blanket was gone."

"I had it thrown out," said Plaid Lady. She opened the door.

"Thrown out!" cried Jean, horrified. "That's somebody's bedroom, some poor guy . . . but it could be a girl, couldn't it . . . some poor person slept there every night. Some poor person came home to the blue blanket."

Cold air drifted up to Ian. A poem that had frightened him as a child wailed in his head. *Ladybug, ladybug, fly away home. Your house is on fire. Your children will burn.*

He closed his eyes and leaned into the wall. Below, they seemed to have paused by the open door. As if from a distance, he heard Jean say, "You could've at least left her a note."

"Delbert Joe is *not* a female," snapped Plaid Lady. "According to the police, he wanders the neighborhood with a shopping bag. When it gets

131

real cold, the police arrest him so he can sleep warm in jail. I didn't want the public having to step over a blue blanket." Ian heard a note of panic spread through her voice. "This place opens for a members' preview next week!"

"It was *his* blanket, Sam," protested Jean.

"That's the price you pay when you don't take responsibility for yourself," said Plaid Lady sharply. They had started to move away from the door as it closed, and Ian had to listen hard to hear what followed as they disappeared out of his line of vision. Was Plaid Lady Sam?

"Which brings to mind your future. Any idea what that will be without a high school diploma?"

Ian couldn't decipher Jean's reply. But the weak sound of her voice had a plaintive note, like kittens mewing.

He returned to the roof hut, but the volunteers assembling kites were silent except for a few complaints. "These strings are totally tangled," or "John David! Have I got the head on the wrong end?" or "Somebody hold the tail while I unravel the whole thing." Occasionally, Ian heard the rumble of the cherry picker as it was moved, then the hum of machinery lifting the box to the ceiling. Sometimes, Movie Star Guy's voice came sharply to him, separated only by the opaque glass ceiling. There were a few exclamations from way below.

"I've lost an antler," or "Look at this!" or "Ouch!" Nothing that gave any strong clues, only that progress was slowly taking place. So slowly it made him sleepy. He climbed down from the roof and visited the Assistant Prosecutor's office on the second floor to watch the outside steps below for Jean and Plaid Lady. He leaned against the sill, half hidden by a musty drape, and didn't realize he had fallen asleep standing up until he was awakened by voices.

Plaid Lady and Jean were below, carrying between them a huge sign on a standard. When they were lost from view, he heard one of the front doors open. He longed to help them with their load, hold open the door. Guide the way.

He slipped back to his stairway post and was rewarded by part of another conversation. The two had paused in the main hallway, out of sight, but clearly audible.

"It's time you had an interesting job here," Plaid Lady was telling Jean. "Bone up on kites, will you?" Were they sitting on one of the long benches lining the hallway, Ian wondered.

"Oh?" questioned Jean.

"Sue is bringing a whole slew of kite books for KIDlift and a lot of kite-making materials and equipment. I think you ought to train the docents for the kite show."

Now Jean's voice squealed like an alarmed cat. "Me?!"

"Yes, you." Plaid Lady's voice sounded wickedly teasing. But then she said seriously, "We have docent volunteers of all ages and types. They will be taking tour groups through the exhibition and explaining everything about the kites. But first, *you* will have to explain everything to *them.*"

There was silence. It was heavy with something Ian couldn't identify. He sniffed. Fear?

Plaid Lady continued, "We have a group of city fathers—and mothers—coming in tomorrow after-noon to check us out. You can practice on them. So bone up."

"Tomorrow!" Jean was the alarmed cat again. "Tomorrow?"

"I have the utmost faith in you," said Plaid Lady. "But first, get on the phone with city maintenance. We need someone to fix those damned clocks. Remind them, we're going to have the public milling through here in a little over a week—*their* public. When we open at ten every morning, I don't want the clocks saying eleven."

"*That* I can do," said Jean. Ian heard them move down the hallway toward Plaid Lady's office. "The other—I don't know . . ."

"You can do anything, my girl," said Plaid Lady firmly, her voice trailing back to Ian. "Anything."

He was no longer tired. He sat down on one of the scattered chairs, digesting what he had heard. A new word: *docent.* Jean had to study kites to train docents. Docents. The word had a religious sound. Or the sound of perfume. Plaid Lady thought Jean could do anything. Why wasn't Jean in high school anymore? Why were things so hard for her?

But late in the afternoon, from the roof hut he heard Jean below among the volunteers. She sounded confident as a teacher.

"I'm going to entertain you all while you are slaving away with the kites." Her voice came from the far end of the room. "These posters will accompany the show. Some will be in the hallway; some will be in this room with the kites. Just listen to this." Her voice grew louder.

"A kite's essentials are three: first, a wing surface shaped or contrived so that it gains lift from the breeze; second, a line or tether that keeps the kite from being blown helplessly away; and, third, a bridle that holds the face of the kite at an angle to the wind.

"A bridle! Like on a horse!" exclaimed Jean. "That's control!" Now her voice faded a little. Ian guessed she was wandering around the room as she read. He tried to picture her. The poster she held would be one of the framed ones he'd seen stacked up against the judge's bench last night.

They had seemed difficult so he hadn't tried to read them.

"The bridle is a critical factor. It establishes the kite's angle of incidence or the angle of attack, and for some kites, the attachment of the bridle must be adjusted from time to time as the strength of the wind varies.

"Hhoooh! It's really a science. The angle of incidence. That's what sailboats use, and parachutes, to harness the wind."

"Airplanes," piped a woman's sweet voice.

"And birds," contributed a man.

And dragons, thought Ian. Dragons use the angle of incidence to get them where they're going.

He could hear Jean click-clacking through the stack of frames.

"That's a delta kite, John David," she said gleefully, "the one you're putting up. You can tell by the fin underneath. And the line you fly with— that's a tether."

She wandered around reading. Ian learned about California kitemakers. And the origin of the kite. He admired Jean's reading; she never stumbled over big words or lost track in a long sentence. She has the gift of gab, too, he thought.

Ian learned that kites have been around nearly four thousand years. He heard explanations of fighter kites, how their lethal tails were encrusted with broken glass to saw through another kite's tether. Kite fighting had been an honored national sport in Japan, where traditions and secrets of building and flying were passed on in families through generations. Great rivalries existed for hundreds of years.

Jean read each framed poster aloud to the crew of volunteers and, unknown to her, an increasingly fascinated Ian. The information anchored easily in his mind.

"Thank you, Jean." It was the quiet, measured voice of a lady. "It makes more sense out of what we're doing." She laughed pleasantly. "I didn't know this was a parafoil."

A patient-sounding man asked Jean to read some of the posters again.

Not one of them knows, thought Ian, smiling to himself, that right above their heads, someone else is learning about kites.

That night he bedded down in the gallery. The cherry picker loomed like a shadowy fortress. A few remaining benches, on which some small kites waited to be hung, were against the walls.

He chose to sleep on the floor beneath the King of Dragons, hoping to fly again, wondering if, now that he knew something about these kites, his dragon dream would come once more. Would it be changed? He hoped not. He wanted to fly farther into the dream. He wanted to catch up with the other dragon. There was something he needed to find out.

Above him, faintly lit by the exit lights at the doors, the shadowy shapes of a multitude of kites stirred as if by some gentle breath. He did not feel fear or loneliness. A host was guarding him—a horse with wings, tigers, a great fish against a wall swimming with a red-cheeked man, a silken eagle, butterflies and ladybugs and stars, flowers and great snakes, warriors with fierce eyes, pirates and pandas, devils and cranes. A mysterious lady spread cloth arms toward him, a kite like a long box glowed pale near the window. And the dragon, the magnificent King of Dragons gathered them all in a hovering army.

To make sure no one could come in unexpectedly, he had locked the doors to the gallery. He put his belongings under one of the benches. But it was not these precautions that lent such lovely comfort to his new sleeping place. He smiled into the dusky shifting atmosphere of the ceiling, where the shapes of the King of Dragons and his throng kept watch.

His sense of safety was so strong, he did not dream at all but slept deeply and woke in the gray wash of morning with a feeling of well-being he had not known since he had lived with his grandmother.

He lay there savoring the day's beginning and noticed that the great red head of the phoenix, which had faced the center of the room last night, had now turned itself toward the window—like a sentinel. Its long, long tail nearly brushed the rail of the jury box. The King of Dragons had not moved; he still tipped his fierce head toward Ian.

Ian sat up, his glance roaming among the mass of kites. Some were propped against the judge's bench, still awaiting their spot in the spectacle. He rose and walked around the room, reading for himself the descriptions and histories in the framed posters that were now hung in a row on one wall. They weren't as difficult to read as he had thought, especially since he'd heard Jean's reading. But he longed for the library dictionary. Here was a photo of a man named Alexander Graham Bell, an inventor or something, who had built a gigantic kite of many wind cells called the Tetrahedron. Ian sounded the word out. Then he tried to locate some of the kites he had just read about.

The clock in the gallery said 7:30. Plaid Lady usually came in when the clocks read 8:00; other people arrived about an hour later. There was plenty of time to return to the second floor and get himself situated for the day ahead.

He unlocked the gallery doors and collected his

belongings from beneath the bench. Everything, including his backpack, he had wrapped in Birthday Boy's coat and tied it with packing string he'd found among the crates.

Walking down the long hallway past the main doors, he was halted in his tracks by a brightly painted door banked by windows on either side. Crisp red letters rode wavy paths of blue on the windows. *KIDlift,* said the lettering. Only yesterday, you could make out through the windows a bare, drab room with wires of some kind coming out in the middle of the floor. How had he missed this new look? The KIDlift room was across from the side entrance where Plaid Lady used her key in the morning. Near his stairway post. And now he remembered seeing people arrive with brushes and paint cans yesterday afternoon. They wore old loose clothing. Ian's father would never have allowed Ian to wear clothes that old and ragged.

Ian couldn't see clearly what changes had taken place inside this room until he opened the door, leaned in, and flipped on the light switch. He took a quick look. The blue path wove from wall to wall around the room. Above the blue danced the red letters: KIDlift—over and over.

At one end of the room were clustered boxes and tables and chairs, all painted blue or red, drying on newspaper. Piled on the floor were baskets filled with crayons, pencils, notepads, colored paper, and a fat jar of rulers and scissors. A Christmas tree stood in one corner. Silvery letters on the wall above labeled it WISHING TREE. A Wishing Tree. Something bright and exciting was happening to this room, too.

With a glad feeling of anticipation, Ian climbed the stairs to stow his gear and station himself for the day's watch.

"There's too much fun in store for me," he prophesied aloud. Then to his father he promised, "I won't let it make me foolish."

CHAPTER TWELVE

Discovery

Twenty-four dollars. He smoothed out the bills on the floor. Outside the little arched windows, a gray morning promised snow. Two tens made twenty, plus four ones. Over the past few weeks he had become really good at adding and subtracting. Now he counted out the change in his pocket, twenty-five, thirty, forty, another quarter—that made it sixty-five—and three pennies. Twenty-four dollars and sixty-eight cents. That was all he had left of Birthday Boy's money. Last Saturday he had had about thirty-five dollars. How had he managed to squander more than ten dollars since then? After his eating splurge a week ago, he had promised himself he would keep his wits about him.

Despair sent a sluggish ache through him. He

had been frivolous and stupid. He had eaten dinner at La Potageria on Tuesday, of all the dumb
things, and once had spent money on a round-trip
bus fare and lunch at the mall. He had to get hold
of himself. True, he had managed to get some
warm gloves from the attendant at the lost-and-
found booth. "My mom says to check for my gloves
I lost." He had wondered if the attendant noticed
how toneless and fake his voice sounded. But she
had pulled out a big box and he spotted the
padded gray ones right away. "Those're mine." His
spontaneous eagerness was real, and the deceived
girl had been pleased to give someone their lost
gloves.

But he shouldn't have rewarded himself for the
gloves with the taco and a Coke. *Water is the only liq-
uid needed to survive.* How much had that Coke
cost? More than a dollar at the mall. More than
groceries for a whole meal. Most of the time, he
had shopped carefully for supplies at Horrebs and
had dined on free samples there in the evening.
But he had to be even more careful. Had to.

Thinking about the money made him hungrier.
He hadn't had his breakfast yet and his supplies
needed replenishing. He would visit Horrebs
again. Saturday was a big shopping day. A man in a
tuxedo played the piano and there were lots of free
samples.

He was recognized now by some of the check-out clerks, though he tried to use a different one each time.

"Your mom's lucky," one of the friendlier clerks told him a few days ago, "to have such a responsible son."

Horrebs was filled with shoppers. There were a lot of food samples. He filled up on apple slices, fresh pineapple chunks, broccoli with dip, several tiny cups of apple juice, and cheese-topped crackers. A nice lady dishing up pizza seemed to like to feed kids. She smiled at him and gave him a plate with four slices of Sooper-Dooper sausage pizza, double cheese, instead of the usual single piece. He bought his groceries—peanut butter, raisin bread, oranges in a net, a large bag of unsugared generic cereal loops he could eat by the handful, milk (half-price sale on 2 percent dated today). Then he chose a checkout line with a new clerk. But as he was leaving with his purchases and a full stomach, the friendly clerk called over from the next check-out station, "Say hello to your mom for me."

Ian realized she had actually imagined a mother for him and now believed she had seen him with that mom. It was easy to help people see what they wanted to see. He thought that next time he would tell her, "My mom says hello." This idea warmed him. His depression was lifting.

It was midafternoon when he arrived back at his building on foot. It had snowed while he'd been shopping, a light layer joining sidewalks to buildings to trees. He stood for a while in a little snow-covered meridian across from the main entrance, his arms around the sack of groceries. He checked the parking lot for cars, the windows for lights. No one appeared to have gone in since he'd left.

He had not been able to think of a way to signal his father. But he was certain his dad would search the place for him. His father needed his coat, too.

He stood there studying the Hall of Justice, his feet growing cold and wet. In just a couple of weeks the old building had been really transformed. There was no place to leave a sign for his dad. Too many people were now drawn to look at the building. Pedestrians stopped; cars slowed down.

Over the main entrance twinkled the red-and-silver ARTlift marquee that Movie Star Guy had built. The red banners, hanging from the roof, drew attention to the great windows, where tempting glimpses of the kites were framed. The top of the grand old building was outlined in Christmas lights.

Bold red-and-black signs, facing the street, announced:

OPENING SATURDAY
NOVEMBER 21
KITES! KITES! KITES!
THE MAGIC OF FLIGHT
PLUS
HOLLYSHOP CHRISTMAS BOUTIQUE
Gifts and Ornaments by Michigan Artists
AND
KIDlift
Creative Activity for Young Folks
through
JANUARY 3
Bring the Whole Family—Hot Cider and Finger Foods

Who could resist, thought Ian. But with the advent of crowds milling through the Hall of Justice, the chances of someone straying to the second floor increased. Twice, when the Lady Leader had brought groups of people for a tour, she had invaded the second floor. Luckily the elevator made a detectable noise. He had been able to exit to the roof. Once people started visiting the kites and the gift shop, kids might be tempted to climb the stairs. He would have to add to his strategy for avoiding discovery.

He realized the cold in his feet at the same time he remembered the happy thought he had gone to sleep with. KIDlift. He would visit that bright inviting room and inspect it more carefully.

As he crossed the little drive in front of the building, he noticed tire tracks in the snow and a square space near the curb where no snow had fallen. A car had been there, parked, then left. Not Plaid Lady. She always parked at the end of the drive. What appeared to be a couple of sets of footprints marched in two uneven lines from the side door and down the wide steps. One pair of feet was considerably larger than the other. Footprints. He had not had to worry till now about covering his footprints. With deliberate care, he placed the tips of his toes in the wide part of the biggest footprints and, clutching his groceries, hobbled across the drive, up the walk, and gingerly climbed the stairs to the concourse where there was no snow. Then he checked to see if his halting progress had been observed. There were a few people on the sidewalk and cars moving along the street, but no one appeared to have noticed him.

Ian entered cautiously, using his key at the hidden side door. No sounds came to his listening ears. The building was empty. KIDlift was so close he decided to visit before he stowed his supplies on the second floor.

When he turned on the KIDlift lights, bright kid-color burst into bloom. Blue and red tables and counters now sectioned the space into cozy alcoves. There were lots of blue and red chairs, all kid sized, some low to the ground for really small children, others higher for grown ones. Leaving the door ajar, he cautiously entered.

A large blue-and-red box had been placed upside down over the place where wires had been coming out of the floor. On it were the supplies he'd seen earlier—rulers, pencils and crayons, colored paper, scissors. There was a basket filled with fabric scraps, another of rubber bands, and several rolls of twine.

It didn't look like Plaid Lady's style, so it must have been somebody else with a key who had been here. He paused in his delight, listened carefully. "I won't get foolish," he said aloud, reminding his father, and he left the bright room to check the halls and the gallery.

Satisfied he was alone, he returned to wander among the KIDlift alcoves, noting a kite-making section with kite examples and how-to drawings; a poetry-writing area, where, according to an outline fixed to the wall, you could write a poem that began with "Kites seem to be . . ." and end it with ". . . but I think they are . . ." There was a science alcove with a plugged-in fan facing the ceiling where you were encouraged to test your kites by flying them in wind created by the fan.

In a box marked TAKE ONE, Ian took a folder that explained KIDlift. There was a box next to it marked DONATIONS. Ian was tempted to put a quarter in, but his father's voice whispered in his ear.

He stood in front of the Wishing Tree. Taped to the wall was an example of how to make a little kite, color it, write down a wish on its face, and hang it on the tree. Wishing wasn't something his father encouraged. Once, during the first few weeks of being with his dad, Ian had been following behind him down the street. It was summer, warm and blue-skied. Ian had been hopping, adjusting his stride so that he didn't step on sidewalk cracks. If he stepped on a crack, he wouldn't get his wish, which, at the moment, was for an ice-cream cone.

"Why are you walking funny?" his father had asked him. Ian had felt embarrassed, but he told him about making wishes happen by stepping over the cracks.

"Only helpless people make wishes. Don't let useless wishes hobble your gait. If you want ice cream, figure out how to get it."

Ian had spent some serious time trying to figure out how to get ice cream without any money, without any grandmother, without any refrigerator. He did not get an ice-cream cone that day.

Now he stared at the Wishing Tree with scorn and longing before he turned away.

Five plump blue pillows were invitingly arranged

in a corner by a red bookcase against the wall. The books were mostly about kites, some about airplanes, a few on the art of paper folding—origami.

After listening to Jean read aloud to workers in the gallery, he had been especially fascinated when, the following day, with the confidence of a teacher, Jean had explained about box kites and delta kites and kites called sleds, fighter kites, and survival kites used by the army. Now was his chance to find out even more, to see pictures and diagrams.

He sat on a blue pillow and pulled a weighty book, *The Complete Book of Kites and Kite Flying,* into his lap. How long he was there he couldn't say, but he was deep into a chapter called "Odd Uses of Kites," when a familiar sound clicked a warning: Plaid Lady's key in the side door.

He leaped to his feet, jammed the book back onto the shelf, and grabbed his groceries. Fast, fast, his brain working. Rush across to the light switch, flip it off. Or flee immediately by the back exit?

At that very moment, a whole herd of people came through the main doors in a straggling group and milled into the hallway. Ian recognized, through his panic, some of the people who worked in HollyShop. Then the side door heaved slowly inward, displaying Plaid Lady's shoulder. She was puffing and cursing, pushing a box with her foot. Instinctively, Ian put down his bag, hurried to the side door, and pulled it all the way open.

"May I help?" he inquired breathlessly. *The safest place from danger . . .*

"Ah, a godsend! To whom do you belong?" asked Plaid Lady.

"I'm here to help," stammered Ian. He picked up Plaid Lady's box, then leaned against the door to hold it open for her.

"My mom said to help." His brain whirled efficiently. Lies as true as breathing exhaled from his mouth. "She works for Grand River. She's on a committee."

"Museum League?" asked Plaid Lady. "Who let all you guys in?"

"Oh, Sam," said a blond woman hurrying down the hall, "that door that won't shut right; it was open."

"I see you've checked out KIDlift already," remarked Plaid Lady wryly. "We are going to need help in there supervising the little monsters." She looked at Ian. "What committee is your mom on?"

"I don't know the name," said Ian. "It's for the city."

"Well, we've got a zillion committee ladies," said Plaid Lady. "What're you good at?"

He was in. "I know about kites," said Ian in a

burst of true enthusiasm. "I could talk to the little kids about kites."

"What's your name? These aren't regular kites, you know," said Plaid Lady. She *was* Sam then.

"Yes, I know," said Ian. "My name is Ian and I know about delta-wing kites and box kites and parafoils; I know how to tell a bowed kite from a flat kite. I know about fighter kites with the crushed glass on their tails—or razor blades—to chop the strings from other fighters." Should he have made up another name for himself? Too late now.

Plaid Lady was eyeing him with interest. From straight on, she looked younger and her eyes were full of humor. He had to keep her from asking more about where he belonged.

"Japanese fighters are said to be the fastest, but the Koreans say theirs are. I know about the Hargrave box kite and how he invented it so the military would be able to observe the enemy. I know kites were invented in China around 2,000 B.C. and only rich people could have them because they were made of silk and silk was very expensive." Information gleaned in a few hours over two days spilled from him. "I know about how a Chinese emperor sent his son to safety during a battle by lifting him across a river with a kite."

Plaid Lady's eyebrows lifted. "More than I know. And where, pray tell, did you learn all this?"

Ian gulped. But he could tell the truth. "Books." Relief was making his head float away from his body. Did it show on his face? The rest of his body might fold up into the lightness. Could he work through to the other side of dizzy? *Stay calm. When the demon is on you . . .* He took a breath, froze his mind. "There are books that tell you this stuff." He watched her eyes. "In the library," he added.

"Well first, why don't you help me with the box you are already holding? We'll figure out later where you fit in."

Ian quieted his breathing. As he carried the box toward Plaid Lady's office, his canniness returned; his head came back to his body. He remembered in time to pretend he didn't know the way. "How much farther?" he asked, straining with the box.

His mind was now ticking in the old way. He'd have to retrieve his groceries. He thought he'd heard the peanut butter roll out of the bag as he'd hurried to greet Plaid Lady at the door. *Attack is the best method of defense.*

✧⇒◯⇐✧

The doctor was wearing casual clothes as if he'd just been golfing.

"You can't recall your father at all?"

"I think I used to know," said Patient 227. "I have a

vague image: His face was always sunburned. He was strong. Physically. That's about all."

During his first few visits to the psychiatrist, Patient 227 had talked mostly about the war—jungles and rice paddies, simple villages filled with hidden danger, the fear. In a voice made of stone, he arduously carved out stone sentences while the doctor listened. At least, he thought the doctor listened. Hard to tell while lying on your back laboring with memory. He spoke of fear and of dead men: Ralsky and Swartout and Stern—and Will. He spoke of fear and the wounded, the missing—Skunk and Reefer. He spoke of fear and the prisoner compound, the broom whisking out the code messages, the hot box for punishment. He told of how, when he came back home, he couldn't go into the woods beyond the house—woods he'd played in as a boy. Woods he knew as well as his mother's face. He had spoken about these things to other doctors over the years. He had it down to a routine. He didn't feel a thing in the telling. He didn't sweat or cry anymore.

"Then you remember your mother?"

"Oh, yes. Red hair, even when she got old. She loved that damn old farm. There was a farm. And those chickens. I can still hear her making those squawky-scolding sounds to them."

"You didn't like the farm, then?"

"No," said Patient 227, then thought. "Well, that's not right. I liked it enough. It just . . . it never used me *up. At night I felt restless, wasted. She got real frustrated with me, Ethel."*

"Ethel?"

"My mom—Ethel was her name."

"Do you think your mother loved you?"

"What the hell kind of question is that?" He lunged up from the couch into a sitting position. He looked the golfing doctor in the eye. Sighed. "I think she loved me as much as she could." He remembered the fall from the porch, her arms around him. "Yeah, she loved me. She really loved the boy though. Liked having him around . . ."

"The boy?"

Then it was real. He'd said it. He had a son and he remembered him and the kid wasn't a baby anymore, didn't live with his grandmother in the ancient farmhouse that had been in the Bayless family for generations. Old scenes flashed through his mind like a runaway reel, then slowed down. An image of a serious, hopeful face. Dark red hair. The boy was nine or ten. Eleven? A thin, tall kid— and smart. What was his name? Where was he now?

Then he realized that, for the past ten minutes, he had been talking about his mother in the past tense.

"My mother is dead," he told the doctor. He felt a pang of fresh loss. A surprise of tears welled up in his eyes. She would never know who he truly was, would never help the boy grow up—whoever the boy was, wherever the boy was.

CHAPTER THIRTEEN

New Kid on the Team

He was actually walking around in the gallery in broad daylight with other people there. At first Ian could hardly focus because of the sensation. Little bursts of a laugh kept erupting unbidden from his lips. When he tried to control this, the light-headed feeling threatened again.

Plaid Lady had liked the idea of a kid like him taking school groups on tours of the show. "Educate yourself some more," she had told Ian, and sent him to the gallery.

The last of the kites were being hung. Spy Hat was on the tall machine putting up a small feathered eagle, helped by a serious-looking lady and a smoothly pretty girl about Jean's age. He looked up at them, tried to keep his mouth from falling open at this turnabout, the strangeness of being

the one below. They smiled briefly at him and continued working. He wondered where Jean was and
quelled a rush of panic. He was in. And the gift of
gab was still his.

After a silent greeting to the King of Dragons,
Ian pretended to carefully examine the grand dis-
play he already knew. High happiness began to
sing in his veins. It felt dangerous. With great care,
he forced his attention to the papers he held. Plaid
Lady had given him a typed draft of the program
guide she was going to have printed. It was difficult
for him to tackle—the small type, the crossed-out
parts, scrawled handwriting in the margins, and
many words he didn't know. He longed for the
library dictionary. Plaid Lady didn't even have one
in her office. She must know all the words. The
momentary despair at his lack of schooling was as
bad as the light-headedness. So he made himself
examine the exhibit itself.

Under the new and special lighting of the
gallery, Ian began to notice things he hadn't
before. The Portuguese kite was constructed
mostly of newspaper; the date he made out on one
of them was *Outubro 17, 1965*. The tail was a long
row of newspaper dolls joined at the hands and
feet.

He could feel himself settling down. He moved
on to a bowed silk kite that bore the fine painting

of a powdered and painted man on a white horse flanked by a powerful soldier and a pig-man. They were all led by a dancing monkey in red pantaloons. Who were they, Ian wondered, and where were they going? The program guide listed the kite as "Travel to the West." It was Chinese. He would have to find out more for the little kids.

Movie Star Guy John David was working intently behind the judge's bench on some kind of sound system. Timidly Ian peered over the edge of the platform, but John David was so fixed in his purpose that he only glanced up briefly. "Can you hand me those pliers?" he asked, which Ian did with a rush of joy. He tried to suppress his pleasure but could feel a smile brimming in his face. Peering absently over his little half-glasses, Movie Star Guy hadn't even recognized the gnome.

However, there were so many things Ian had to figure out and fix in his mind that most of his sober control returned. A family, a school. Questions would be asked. Were his clothes clean enough? Would he have to use some of his dwindling funds at the Laundromat? Fortunately he had used the shower only yesterday, spending a long time afterward wiping all the water out with paper towels. But his clothes were none too clean. Even his two pairs of spare underwear, rinsed in the men's room sink, were pretty gray looking.

How would he wash his jeans? The sudden image of himself huddled on a chair inside Birthday's Boy's coat at Suds Yer Duds, naked legs curled up, while his jeans spun around with all the other clothes he owned, horrified him. But he couldn't waste those quarters without washing everything.

Should he give his real last name? It was only a matter of time before Plaid Lady would think to ask. He needed an address and phone number, too. Tonight after everyone had left, perhaps he would try a lot of phone numbers until he found some that didn't answer. Then, maybe he would try them early tomorrow morning until he had isolated numbers no one answered. People went away in winter, his father said. It seemed an awfully complicated plan. His father said the best plans were simple ones. He had two days to find a house where people were gone. Plaid Lady said she didn't need the volunteer form filled out and signed by a parent until Thursday—and would he be allowed to help with the members' preview reception on Friday? Ian had already given himself a mother. Should he give himself a father? Perhaps one who traveled.

School. What school would he go to? Should he use the name of his old school where Miss Lusk had been his second-grade teacher? That was too far away, in another county. He would tell the home-schooling lie he had told the children's librarian in the past.

"Too bad you're too young for working papers," Plaid Lady said when he returned to her office and handed her back the typed program. He kept his body held away in case his clothes had a smell. But she didn't seem to notice if he smelled or not. "We need people to staff the ticket desk."

Her real name, he reminded himself, was Sam. She proffered a box with doughnuts in it. "Yesterday's treats, but . . ." She bit into one. "Not bad." She smiled at Ian.

Ian took a doughnut and a yip of laughter popped out of him—as if he were committing an embarrassing social error. Last night he had swiped a doughnut from this very box. He stifled further yips by eating the doughnut.

"We might be able to provide token payment— like with baby-sitters. They don't need working papers. I expect you'll be out of school for the holidays during the busy time here."

"I'm in home-schooling," said Ian, brushing sugar along with an unbidden smile from his mouth. There. School was taken care of. "But my mom allows this kind of work—volunteer work. I learn a lot." He felt a momentary pride in his use of *volunteer.* He'd never said the word he'd been overhearing for weeks.

"Your mom is a woman after my own heart," crowed the Plaid Lady called Sam. "If you like, borrow some of the kite books in KIDlift when you leave. Do you need a ride? Is your mom picking you up? We're not going to stick around here all day."

"I'm meeting my mom downtown. I can walk. Thanks." Ian turned to go. Then stopped. "Why isn't there anything in that program thing about how old the kites are? Like, the Chinese phoenix must be old, but the square dancers from Canada look new."

"Good idea!" exclaimed Sam. "Good thinking! Thank you, Ian. Maybe we'll give you that research job. Got any more inspirations?"

"No." Ian was startled. He felt the yipping laugh sneak up on him again and hurried out of her office. It hadn't been an idea, an inspiration. It had been a question. He had only wanted an answer. What was it his dad had said about answers being found in the right question? Maybe ideas were found that way, too.

Since no one was in the main hall and no one was at the entrance foyer, he slipped up the stairs to the second floor, stayed out of sight for an hour or so until he was certain everyone had left, and had his meal: peanut butter on bread, milk, and a handful of cereal. Feeling well in control, he left the building and set out to find a house.

Most of the snow had melted in the sun, which was now setting; shadows stretched long on the wet streets. Glad of Birthday Boy's coat in the gathering cold, he walked nearly half an hour to a good residential area across town. It was a neighborhood of handsome, comfortable houses. *People live here who are rich enough to go south in winter*—his dad's voice in his head.

He strode up and down the blocks until he found a house whose mailbox overflowed with mail that looked like mostly catalogs. He memorized the name, Gibbons, and number, 87½ Wolnough. On Freemont Street he found another house with the same burdened mailbox. Foxmore, 207. He wished he'd remembered a pencil and paper, but he said the names and numbers over and over in his mind until he got back to Plaid Lady Sam's office. Then he looked up the phone numbers. Neither answered when dialed. Gibbons had an answering machine that asked you to leave a message, so he chose Foxmore. Ian Foxmore, 207 Freemont Street, 555-6702.

He was studying the Finnish kite with the eerie, fluttering tails. Monday had rolled around and only he, Movie Star Guy, and Plaid Lady Sam were at work this early. He had just tipped his head to study the kite from a different angle, when a familiar, low voice startled him from the doorway.

"It's called the Djinn. It's like a ghost; it's from Finland." It was the voice from which he'd learned kites while standing on a steel grating above this room. He turned. Jean walked toward him with her long pigeon-toed gait. She was not smiling and although she seemed unaware of his secrets, he felt as if she could read his mind.

"Those transparent eyes let the landscape show through when it's flying, which gives it a really weird look. It's made by . . ." She halted and stared at him. ". . . like the landscape is showing through yours right now."

Then she laughed. "I'm not that strange or beautiful, am I?" Ian couldn't stop staring at her.

"I'm Jean Neary. My mother runs this place and the museum across town, too."

"I know," said Ian in a voice so swallowed and low he could barely hear himself. Jean seemed pleased with the answer and his obvious awe.

"You mean you know my name or you know my mother runs things? Which?"

"Both."

"Oh," said Jean. She appeared relieved.

From this new vantage point, head on, she seemed different. Her face was round; her skin creamy. When she moved, a lovely slanting shine ran up and down the dark length of her hair. Way-too-large clothes made her look elfin, though she was tall. She had a cleanness that made him glad he had suffered, naked and nervous, tented inside Birthday Boy's coat, at Suds Yer Duds while all his clothes washed and dried. Although he had gotten a few glances from three tired woman there early Sunday morning, no one said anything to him.

Jean pulled back and looked at Ian the way you would a painting. "Hey. You're the one Sam is raving about. The godsend. Sam said you had hair the color of an English riding saddle." Her bright laugh spun toward him. "It *is* that kind of red, sort of burnished like a saddle. Ian. Is it Ian? I thought you would be a little kid."

"I'm eleven," said Ian.

"You look older—like a high school freshman, maybe."

"I'm home-schooled." The lie had grown very comfortable.

"That's really cool!" said Jean. She seemed eager to find out more about home-schooling, but Sam came marching into the gallery before she had a chance to ask Ian anything else.

"I'm thinking of doing Clonlara schooling," Jean whispered to him. "I'd love to talk to you later."

"Right now, Jean," said Plaid Lady Sam, "let's hear what you'll tell the docents when they assemble tomorrow morning for the first training session." She had a pencil behind each ear and her hair had a rumpled look. She gave a large worried sigh. "We'll have docent training Tuesday and Wednesday. Then we'll have a run-through on Thursday when a high school group from Central arrives for a tour in the morning."

Jean's easy calm seemed to desert her. "Central kids are coming here?"

"Don't worry. Your docents will do that tour. You will observe them to see where they need sprucing up. I will observe you observing." Sam gave her short bark of a laugh. "We open Friday for a members' preview and reception. We gotta be beautiful by then."

"But kids from Central?" asked Jean. "Which kids? Which class?" She seemed truly worried.

"I don't know that," said Plaid Lady Sam. "Probably Wolfson's English class. What I do need to know is your strategy. Where are you going to start with the training?"

"My brain just went dead," said Jean. "Give me a minute."

"We can do that," said Sam. "How about you, Ian? Where would you start? What would you tell these innocent people?"

Ian was dismayed when Jean faltered, when her face went blank. A warm, strong feeling spread through him. He could help.

"I'd just start at the door where everyone comes in," said Ian. Part of the gift of gab was thinking on your feet. "I'd just tell them a little bit about each kite. I'd . . . I'd go around the room and talk about the kinds of kites. They could write it down, if they want. They should bring paper and a pencil."

Facing the ceiling, Ian walked beneath the vast assembly of kites. "I'd ask their opinion of certain kites, what they liked about them." He stopped beneath the King of Dragons. "Then I'd tell them that they should start their tours with their favorite kite, the one they really like."

"Brilliant," said Sam. Jean had turned her lovely, cream-skinned face toward him, eyes surprised.

"I'd give them homework," continued Ian with growing confidence, "like copies of your program to study later."

"Jean?" asked Sam.

"I agree," said Jean. "What can I add? It's really cool. Maybe Ian and I should work together training the docents?" She turned her large brown eyes toward the older woman. Ian thought they had a sad, worried look. "That way you can observe me observing Ian the godsend—observing the docents."

Plaid Lady Sam smiled. "Good," she said. "That's one more thing I won't have to worry about." As she turned back to her office, she reminded them, "Better get the whole exhibit under your belts now. I put some info printouts of Sue's on the bench by the back wall. Someone else can go pick up lunch, Jean."

Jean made a funny face at Ian, but then she blew out a sigh and gathered the information papers from the bench.

"Sue is the education director. She's very smart and creative and organized." She waved the papers at Ian. "You can trust this information; there's not a lot of junk talk to use up space."

They spent the next several hours studying the show together. Ian was buoyed up by the tall girl's casual acceptance of his role in helping her. She seemed to need him—in the same sort of way his father needed him.

She read aloud from the information papers. Ian wrote down dates for Plaid Lady to include in her printed program. At one point Jean suggested that they take a break and go look for the cells where criminals had been held while awaiting their court case. Ian made his first mistake when he said, "They're locked." He knew when he said it that he'd goofed, and when Jean turned an inquiring face, he said hastily, "I forget who told me that."

Foolish. Foolish. He should not relax so comfortably into the pleasure of this girl's company.

"What's in the glass cases?" he asked to distract her. He'd discovered she was easily distracted.

"Vitrines," said Jean. "The cases are called vitrines." Jean seemed to totally lose interest in the locked cells. Enthusiasm livened up her voice. "Come see. There are kites made of postage stamps. Japanese. And other tiny, tiny kites."

When Sam came into the gallery bearing a lunch of tuna fish sandwiches, tomato soup, and two Cokes, Ian was stunned to note it was almost two-thirty by the clock on the wall—one-thirty in real time.

"Treat's on me," said Sam. "You two have been working pretty hard."

Stay calm. Don't get foolish. Eat slowly. In a steady voice he said, "Thank you."

They sat on the floor beneath the King of Dragons and ate their lunch together. Jean told him about dropping out of school, about her mother getting her a job in the executive dining room of Paulson-Regina Foods Corporation downtown.

"My mom has pull," said Jean. "She knows everybody important in this town." She mimicked her mother: "I don't want a teenage dropout lying around the house." She discussed an ex-boyfriend,

Joshua, in a way that sounded like he was still her boyfriend. She chattered on and finally she asked, "How about this home-schooling stuff? How does it work?"

Ian was startled.

"I read a lot in the library," he said, reaching for the truth.

"Oh," said Jean, disappointed. "That's so lonely."

She lay back on the floor, arms behind her head, and stared unseeing at the kites. "I'd rather read out loud to someone. When I was little, I read my homework to my mom." She was silent for a moment. "That was before she got so wrapped up in her job—so important and all."

Ian tried to think of something good to say to her about home-schooling. *Don't ask for trouble.* He shook off the warnings in his head. "You can always read to me," he offered.

She raised her head and looked at him, brown eyes suddenly happy. "Really?" she asked, and Ian nodded.

That night he did not begin his night's sleep beneath the King of Dragons. Movie Star Guy John David was still working, adjusting lights and the sound system with Spy Hat. From the room for miniature people, Ian could hear the music for the kite show, some swelling and rich, some staccato and foreign sounding. There were sharp rap chants and old-fashioned velvety dance music. He rode the King of Dragons into sleep on waves of music.

When he awakened, the building was silent. He tried to remember his dream. He had the other-world numbness he felt when waking from a strong dream. He caught flashes of color with his memory. Scales? Iridescent, they were. The King of Dragons was sleeping. He had landed and was sleeping on a rock. His scales shone in the sun. All about him others had been sleeping, too. Plaid Lady was sleeping in the grass with her computer. Her computer was sleeping. He looked about in vain for the second dragon. An uneasy feeling came over him. Grass was growing up around the tall yellow cherry picker on whose platform Spy Hat and John David were sleeping. Jean was singing in her sleep. *Fool boy. Fool boy. Fool boy.*

That was what had wakened him! The jabbering sound. Not nearby. Beneath him. He could barely make out the words tumbling together, tripping over each other. He froze his mind, made himself leave his safe room and hurry to the roof hut where he could listen better.

"Miracles, miracles," chattered the demon-ridden voice below. "Better than numbers and sexy baseball cards and greater joke don't forget love. The law is a joke is as love and kindness courteous as best music. Miracles, miracles."

Then he heard the sound of music, Movie Star Guy's music, only turned way up. Loud. The jabbering wove in and out of the music. Then there was some kind of wailing whine, a choking like laughing or sobbing. Ian's skin crawled. Yet this was something that, he knew, had to be taken care of.

Carefully he stole down to Plaid Lady's office. Feeling around, he found the flashlight in her storage room, played its light briefly over her desk to locate the telephone. He'd noticed emergency numbers taped to her phone, police among them. The music was so loud from the other end of the building he could hear it clearly where he was. Keeping the flashlight low, he dialed the number. The call went directly, bypassing the operator.

"Fifth Precinct. Sergeant Betts."

"Someone is playing loud music in the old Hall of Justice," said Ian. "Someone is playing music and singing crazy songs."

Sergeant Betts yelled to someone, "Hey Glen, it's Delbert Joe. In the Hall of Justice. He's been drinking again. Better go on over and say 'nightynight' to him." Then the sergeant spoke back into the phone. "Who is this?"

"The neighbors," said Ian, and hung up.

So it was Delbert Joe after all. Nuttier than a fruitcake. Not a danger at all. And the policeman had spoken about him as if he were a naughty grandfather.

After the police had turned off the music and taken the raving man away, Ian visited the gallery. Delbert Joe had been playing with one of the kites. It was an octopus they had not used. It had been stored in one of the back rooms with a number of kites that wouldn't fit in the "scheme of the show," according to Movie Star Guy.

Very carefully, Ian folded the several long fabric legs of the octopus and returned him to his place in the crate, which listed OCTOPUS inside the lid. He realized that he was automatically cleaning up Delbert Joe's traces and then he knew that was wrong. He removed the octopus, shook him out, and took him back to the floor of the gallery. The police would tell Plaid Lady Sam about Delbert Joe. He should not disturb the evidence.

CHAPTER FOURTEEN

The Partnership

Ian waited outside in Birthday Boy's coat, breath puffing visibly through the cold air. He thought it a good plan, every other morning or so, to be outside waiting for Plaid Lady to let him in. He was eager to see Jean. He'd had an idea after he'd settled down again for the night, this time on the gallery floor beneath the King of Dragons. Why not use the octopus kite and some of the other unused kites still in the back rooms? They could hold them up, maybe pull them through the air— let people get close to them. They'd have to ask permission first.

When Plaid Lady arrived to open the door, the Lady Leader was with her. Mrs. Neary looked at him, her face thick with worry.

"Is Jean here?" she asked him. He shook his

head dumbly. "You haven't seen her?"

"She's usually late," he told her.

The Lady Leader closed her eyes. Plaid Lady Sam looked concerned, too.

"She came in sometime late last night. Her bed was slept in. But she was gone when I got up. She never gets up that early. I don't know where she could have gone."

"She'll turn up," Plaid Lady told Mrs. Neary. "She's disappeared before. She probably went out to meet friends for breakfast and didn't want to wake you." Then Plaid Lady turned to Ian.

"Looks like you'll have to start in alone with the docents when they arrive in about an hour—unless Jean shows up before then." She put her arm around the Lady Leader and led her toward her office, offering suggestions as they went.

"Let's call the kitchen at Paulson-Regina. Maybe she's working breakfast."

In a rush of anxiety, Ian hurried into the gallery, flitted from kite to kite, trying to remind himself, through gathering numbness, of the things he knew. Jean was missing. He was on his own.

But the docents, when they came, were not frightening. They ranged in age from late teens to late seventies. Ian counted seventeen of them, men and women. Some of them clustered near the center icon; some sat on benches reading Plaid Lady's program, which had appeared as if by magic, printed in a bright red pamphlet. Some wandered about, studying the kites. He was surprised to see Movie Star Guy John David among the trainees.

"I understand something about these kites from working with them," said the designer with a charming smile, "but I don't *know* anything about them. I'm here for an education." He tipped his head at Ian, peered over the little half-glasses—tan frames today. "You certainly do look familiar. What's your mom's first name?"

"Wendy," said Ian quickly, thinking hamburgers.

At that moment, Plaid Lady called them together and thanked them for coming. Ian straightened up and breathed easily to quiet the gathering turmoil inside him.

"Most people don't know much about kites," said Plaid Lady Sam. "They don't know the history of kites nor the traditions behind them—nor the many types of kites around the globe. What we're asking of you is to know more than most people, to learn enough to open up new worlds for our visitors."

She put her hand on Ian's shoulder and a fleeting memory of Miss Lusk warmed him.

"Meet our resident kite expert, my godsend, Ian Foxmore."

To Ian's comfort, the docents were pleasant and expectant and not surprised that a boy was the expert. "He's her godson." He caught the whispered mistake among them and smiled. He was in. More than they imagined, he was indeed the resident expert. They obviously didn't know all he knew about kites. And oh yes, he could tell them. There was no danger. There would be no secrets to hide. He was not asking for trouble. He could talk and talk about kites to these obliging people, and no one would need to know the address or school of the kite expert or his mother's first name.

In the hush that followed his introduction, Ian walked to stand beneath the King of Dragons.

"I think it's a good idea to start tours with your own favorite kite. This is mine." He raised his face to look and could feel the faces of the others lift toward the marvelous beast. The gift of gab warmed in him.

"This kite is Chinese. It is not as old as some of the kites in this show—it was made about sixty years ago. Inside its mouth, if you look real close, is a jewel: the Jewel of Wisdom."

The docents clustered eagerly around him. For a brief moment he thought he might tell them what the King of Dragons looked like when you peered down into its body, but he caught himself in time. He moved on, trailed by the attentive docents, to the larger dragon with the ninety-five-foot body of feathered disks. "Dragons are a favorite kind of kite in China." He explained how it took many men to get the disk kite aloft.

From the Chinese kites, Ian took the group to the Japanese kites, the Korean kites, and the kites from Indonesia. He was pointing out the Malaysian hummer kite when Jean's clear voice spun through the air.

"Kites were thought to have originated on the Malay Peninsula because of the offshore winds of tropical islands—and the onshore winds, too. Knowledge of them would have spread north to China, two thousand years ago. These are speculations, of course."

All eyes turned toward the tall girl who, today, along with dragging corduroys and a baby-doll blouse, was wearing a large woolly ski hat. Ian was delighted to see her, this bold, beautiful girl with her own scholarly gift of gab. Why did her eyes seem fearful? Should he introduce her? But he could soon tell, from the docents' response to Jean, that they all knew her, so he simply said, "Jean's a kite expert, too."

They made a good team that afternoon, Jean with her provocative explanations and serious brown eyes, and Ian trying to keep categories of kites in an order the docents could remember. When Jean told the story of struggling to assemble a gorgeous silk kite in the back room and, finally, how it expanded gloriously into many-colored cells like an enormous honeycomb—and they couldn't get it through the doors into the gallery—Ian laughed along with the docents. But then he pointed out that the kite was a parafoil and the wind used the many cells to keep the kite aloft. When Jean drew attention to the silk-screened square dancers on the large Canadian kite, Ian could tell everyone it was a delta kite because of the fin.

"We are a really good team," Jean whispered as the docents were getting ready to leave. Then her eyes grew worried again. Her mother stood in the gallery doorway, and she looked mad.

"In a hat!" snapped Mrs. Neary after the last docent had gone. Her anxiety over her daughter had been replaced by anger. She didn't even ask where Jean had been. "In a hat?! You can't conduct a docent tour in a ragged ski hat."

"Should I have done it this way?" asked Jean with a forced and cheerful calm. She whipped off the hat.

Almost-black hair did not cascade down. Except for a fringe around her face, nothing remained of Jean's long, shiny hair. Behind the edge of fringe, her scalp was a dome, as bald as a wrestler's.

Jean's mother's face was a study in change. It twisted from horror to bewilderment to anger and finally froze.

"Jean, I am very disappointed in you," she said in a voice so cold it sliced the air. She turned and left the gallery.

"But, Mom—" cried Jean desperately. "It's okay. It's a power move. It's shaking up people's expectations so they can see the real me. Joshua says . . ."

"Joshua!" Her mother turned, pounced. "He's behind this freakish move!" Her eyes blazed.

"And who do you think is going to hire this *real* Jean? What will happen, do you imagine, when you show up for work at Paulson-Regina? As for this job—I don't want you doing any tours here looking like an ex-con. You're not representing the museum; you're not representing this family! What are you trying to do to me?"

"I wasn't doing it to you," muttered Jean. "I was doing it to myself." Her mother turned and walked away. "This isn't about you, Mom," said Jean to her mother's back. "Not everything is about you."

But her mother didn't appear to hear her, so low was Jean's voice, and Ian wondered what was true and what was not true.

After her mother had marched silently away, Jean turned to Ian. "My ex-boyfriend did it," she explained, as if he had not heard it the first time.

"Joshua said it would free me from the chains of fad and fashion. He said it would force people to look at the real . . . uh . . . to look at me, Jean, and not my hair or my 'dance with my hair,' as he calls it."

All this information seemed intended to distract Ian from Jean's head. She kept facing him so that all he saw was the cunning fringe this Joshua guy had left around her face. She was talking fast.

"Why'd he do that? Shave your hair off?" asked Ian, not understanding the other reasons.

Jean flushed. "He said he'd always wanted to see how I'd look. It was really a power move. Something external to signal that I don't follow the old rules."

"I liked your hair. I've never seen hair like that—so shiny." He still didn't know the reason for her shorn head. So he persisted. "Why did he want to take it away?"

"Do you like it now?" Jean was almost coy, flirting.

Ian hesitated. "You have a real smooth scalp," he said.

"But don't you like the way I look now?" Jean was teasing.

She is used to getting people to agree, thought Ian. He found himself wanting to please her, too. But he said stoutly, "No. No, I don't like it."

Her large brown eyes seemed to grow larger, browner. Sadder. He wanted to take back his admission.

"Don't lie," his father once said after Ian had overheard him tell Aunt Mildred a big one over a pay phone, saying he was working and, even a bigger lie, that they had a house now. His dad had always tried to keep Aunt Mildred from coming after Ian, so he called her every once in a while with what he called "good news exaggerations."

One time, his dad had told her that Ian was playing Little League, after they had thrown that baseball up and down the hall. Once his dad had asked for Aunt Mildred's recipe for brownies over the phone, as if he were going to bake some, as if he had a stove to bake them in, as if he had a house with a stove to bake anything at all.

But he told Ian, "Don't lie unless the gain is greater than the lie."

That meant you had to weigh so many things, things you could lose against the thing you would become by lying—a coward, a sneak, less of a person than the one you lied to.

If a lie could save your life and keep bad things away, it was a weapon of sorts. But should a person lie to keep another's friendship? Struggling, he found a truth to say.

"It'll grow back," he assured her, relief making his voice lift happily. Then he added another true thing. "It would take a lot more than a haircut to make you ugly."

He was rewarded when some of the sorrow left her face.

CHAPTER FIFTEEN

The Training

She was wearing no hat. Her bald head huddled down inside the collar of her parka like a disturbed turtle. Why had she taken off the hood? Ian watched her from the Assistant Prosecutor's window as she came up the walk. Why was she so early?

She leaned into the wind, took the wide stairs two at a time, then scurried out of view at the landing. He heard a rattle of the latch and her muffled, "Hello? Anybody there?" More frantic rattling. A moment later, he heard her pushing against the faulty door at the main entrance. "Hello? Sam? Somebody!" More heaving against the door. "I'm freezing! Come on-n-n, pul-eese, somebody."

Her voice carried misery. Ian waged a little war with his better judgment, then he hurried down the north stairs to the door, muttering, "It'll be okay, Dad; it's okay."

When he pulled the door open, Jean gave a small shriek. Then she wailed with joy, "Ian. The godsend!"

She had pulled her coat up over her head. He held the door wide, looking into her face. He was almost as tall as she was.

"You'd better come in and get warm," he said. Perhaps, in her gladness, she wouldn't question how he'd gotten inside.

"My hero!" said Jean, laughing with relief, chattering. "I was freezing. I should have never removed my hood. How did you get in? I just noticed Sam's car isn't here yet. Are you a miracle? Can you walk on water? Are you always going to be there at the right moment?"

"Yes," said Ian. Then he asked, "Why did you take off the hood?"

"I didn't think about getting cold. I had no idea hair could keep your head so warm."

Ian followed her into KIDlift.

"Besides, Mom said not to wear the hat. She said, 'You wanted bald. So, do bald!'" Jean made a face. "I knew it would give her a hissy when I unzipped the hood. I left it on her chair so she wouldn't miss it when she came into the kitchen. I left a note: '*I'm doing bald.*'"

They sat in the little KIDlift chairs, knees jutting up. Jean read aloud bits and paragraphs from some of the kite books. They practiced making a few of the simple kites.

"You know," confided Jean, "when I first saw this room, it turned me off. I mean—that sad fake Christmas tree in the corner. It looked tacky to me with those silver Wishing Tree letters on the wall there."

Ian was surprised. Was it because Jean was older? Did things lose their cheeriness when you got old?

"But, you know," she continued, "kids will have a lot of fun here coloring and making kites and cutting things with those safe baby scissors. They will write their little wishes on little kites and hang them on the tacky tree."

"What is 'tacky'?" asked Ian.

"Unconvincing," said Jean. "But it won't be that way at all, will it?" she continued, almost as if talking to herself. "They will read about kites, the older ones, and write kite poems."

"Kite poems?" asked Ian.

"Yes," said Jean. "Over here." She stood and walked over to a small cubicle set off by giant colored blocks. "There are even suggestions here on the wall on how to start, in case you can't think of anything." She sat in a little chair at a blue table.

"Should we write a poem?" asked Jean. Without waiting for an answer, she picked up one of the stubby little pencils from a jar and started off.

"Kites seem to be sort of silly play."

She scribbled this down. Thought a moment. Scribbled some more.

"One end . . . uh . . . holding a paper triangle—holding a bright paper triangle—no. One end holds a flapping paper shape. Yes!

"The other end pulls on a child.

"Now your turn," ordered Jean. "Start with *But I think they are . . .*"

Ian paused. *"I think they are an adventure."* His mind went into the gallery, flitted among the kites.

"They are beetles and fish and snakes.

They pull you out of a dream.

They fly you into a dream.

They are a horse of paper, an eagle of silk.

They are the dragon who is king."

Jean was scribbling madly away: ". . . *a horse of paper, an eagle of silk* . . .

"That is truly beautiful," said Jean when she stopped writing. "You are truly a poet, kite expert, godsend hero."

Ian smiled at her. "Did you write all that down?"

"Yes," said Jean. "And you have to sign your name."

Ian didn't want to sign "Foxmore" and he

couldn't sign "Bayless." He signed "Ian" in large, neat cursive.

"You have the handwriting of a teacher," remarked Jean. "Or an obedient child."

Were his tracks showing again, Ian wondered.

"By the way," asked Jean, as if she'd read his mind. "How did you get in this morning through locked doors?"

"The front door was open," said Ian quickly.

Fortunately, Sam's arrival at that moment changed the subject. The phone was ringing, and Plaid Lady Sam charged in the side door and raced for her office. When Jean and Ian arrived at her doorway, she was barking into the phone.

"This morning, yes. Good. No, they can't be changed from the offices. There's a central box in the basement. It controls all the clocks."

When Sam hung up and saw them in the doorway, she said, "Jean? So early? Was that damn door not closed again? I was sure we checked it. I hear you lost your job at Paulson-Regina. Well, we can keep you both busy here. Lord, I can't get used to that hairless pate, Jean. Your mother seems to have forgiven you already, but I'm holding out for hair. Where's that hat, by the way? It's cold out."

"Mom said not to hide from the experience I went to such great lengths to provide for myself," mourned Jean with an exaggerated sorrowful look.

"Surely she meant indoors, Jean."

"Yeah. I know," said Jean, "but she's punishing me. When I'm lying in the hospital and have all these tubes in me, I can say, 'You told me not to wear a hat.'" Jean practiced gasping for breath, dragging air into her throat. "It'll be pneumonia."

Sometimes, thought Ian, Jean seems very grown up. And other times, she plays baby games. Right now, I am a lot older than she is.

"Well, I don't have time to waste on silliness," said Plaid Lady. "And neither do you two." She stood up and beckoned them toward the hallway and into the little courtroom, HollyShop, filled with gifts and ornaments.

"HollyShop needs help making out price tags for some fresh inventory. Then you can ready yourselves for the docents. You two did a really good job yesterday. Are you still rollin'?"

"Yes, we are," Jean told her. She was quiet and thoughtful, not her usual chatty self, while she and Ian worked with several lady volunteers copying prices on tags and tying them on merchandise in HollyShop.

In the late morning, the docents began to arrive. They put their coats on benches and wandered around in the gallery looking at the kites.

It was Ian's idea to have the docents each do a practice run. "Then everybody keeps learning what everybody else knows about the kites—uhh, well, you know what I mean?"

"Yes," said Jean. "Like we will all share our separate information." Then she explained to the docents that each one would conduct a tour as a kind of rehearsal.

Ian smiled. Right. The team was rollin'.

Some of the docents were shy and took more encouragement than the others. "Remember," Jean said, "you know more about this exhibit than anyone who comes to see it. Think of how you felt when you first walked in. Think of how glad people will be to have you show them stuff."

Now she is really grown up, thought Ian in admiration. No one had even asked about her hair.

Several of the docents had read up on kites and shared information Jean and Ian hadn't learned. John David was awesome. He found something fascinating about nearly every kite in the exhibit and had tidbits to share about the kite makers. His voice filled with a hushed mystery when he guided everyone on a tour.

"All of the kites are my favorites," he confided to Jean and Ian.

The docents left in an excited, talkative group with Jean calling after them, "Remember, tomorrow is the first real tour! Everyone be here!"

She had told Ian that they might just split up

the high school kids—give one or two students to each docent for a personalized tour of the show.

"That way, I don't have to embarrass myself by stuttering or making any dumb moves."

"Why would you?" asked Ian.

"If it's Wolfson's English class, the smart kids," said Jean, "they think I'm a cowardly quitter. If it's the violent hoodlums who beat each other up, they think I'm a cowardly loser. It's making me nervous."

"But you're not any of those things," said Ian. He felt little threads of her misery twisting in the air between them. "You're a very clear person," he added lamely.

"No mystery?" she asked. "Am I all that obvious?"

"You're good at explaining," said Ian, feeling around for her best qualities. He didn't want to tell her she was beautiful. That was too complicated. Finally he said, "You're the best reader I ever heard." And then realized he might have made a mistake. He had been spying from the roof hut when she'd read to the volunteers.

But Jean brightened and seemed not to notice. So Ian offered another opinion.

"I think you have the gift of gab."

The next day, Jean arrived with a feather hung by a thong from one of her fringe locks. She had put on a pretty beaded tunic over a pair of low-slung and dragging purple cords.

It turned out to be Wolfson's English class that arrived, not the school terrorists. Ian noticed that the docents deferred to her in a flattering way. Her ex-Central classmates thought the kite exhibit was "awesome" and "totally cool." Jean seemed cool, too, and in control. Mr. Wolfson shook Ian's hand as they left. After the doors closed behind them, Jean told Ian that their visitors from her old school would pass good gossip back in the high school hallways. She seemed happy, Ian thought.

Jean's good mood continued, and Ian noticed that though the worry in the Lady Leader's eyes didn't completely disappear, she gave Jean a warm hug later.

The next day, Friday, Jean showed up for the members' reception without her usual dragging pants. She was wearing fitted leggings under her beaded tunic, sequined socks, and hiking boots.

"I want to look good for my mom," she told Ian.

Later, when well-dressed men and women began to arrive, Jean's mother laughed and hugged her daughter.

"I suppose I'm getting my just rewards for my hippie days," she kept telling these elegant people. She introduced Jean as "one of the best things I've ever done—my daughter, Jean."

The gallery and main hallway had been decorated with red-and-silver festoons and black balloons. There were tables of dainty sandwiches, tartlets with crab meat, caviar in baby tacos with salsa, hot artichoke dip, and tiny stuffed new potatoes. Beautiful tall glasses held champagne, and there was pink ginger ale punch in little crystal cups.

While Jean toured with some men and women from the business community, Ian took around a group of bent, pretty, bejeweled old ladies.

The shirt Ian had spent four dollars on at the mall's pre-Christmas sidewalk sale felt formal and elegant. He had used part of the docent training pay Plaid Lady Sam had given him. The shirt was not warm but, he had explained last night to the empty gallery—to the King of Dragons—"This is a survival disguise."

The King of Dragons had seemed to sway faintly in approval. Because of this disguise, there would come food and money and unquestioned participation in the ARTlift festivities for at least a month. It was a well-spent four dollars. But Ian felt guilty at his pleasure in the crisp white shirt.

It was somewhat large, a man's shirt, in small. But because he was tall and his arms long, the sleeves fit. He kept the too-large neck open and wore his turtleneck underneath. Jean had told him he looked "really interesting."

It was a wonderful evening. The chandeliers in the main hallway gleamed softly. Odors of food and perfume sweetened the air. People wearing handsome suits, draped tunics, and soft pretty clothing milled around in the gallery and HollyShop, in the halls, carrying champagne glasses, little plates of food. Movie Star Guy John David wore a tuxedo. Spy Hat came with his golden smiling wife and a graceful daughter.

Ian and Jean were kept pretty busy showing and telling. Ian liked the older ladies best. They were so grateful to be shown around. They wore such lovely colors and their hair was so nice and curled and clean. They smiled at him and called him "dear boy" and "young man" and "son." He could have shown them kites forever. He would have given them all a ride on the King of Dragons if they could have come.

And Jean, too. She would love the King of Dragons.

CHAPTER SIXTEEN

The Wishing Tree

There was an enormous amount of food left over from the members' reception. Before the caterers came to clean up, Ian managed to stash a good share of it under the table in Movie Star Guy's studio, which was close to the reception room.

It was more difficult than usual to slip upstairs. People milled continually in the hallways. Finally, under the pretense of heading for the men's room, Ian managed to reach the glassed-in outside stairway and climb to the second floor.

Later, after everyone had left, he transferred the food to the basement refrigerator. It was a chance worth taking. No one seemed to even know the refrigerator was there. The food lasted him into the first week of December, although he developed a terrible thirst from the caviar tacos, which kept him alternately at the drinking fountain and in the bathroom.

That first week in December brought hordes of schoolchildren and their teachers to tour the kite exhibit, make their own kites and poems in KIDlift, and hang Christmas wishes on the Wishing Tree.

December also brought lots of snow. City maintenance kept the driveway and parking lots clear, but Ian and Jean were responsible for shoveling the sidewalk, steps, and wheelchair ramp.

Inside, Jean had to spend part of her time clerking in HollyShop and part of her time helping Sue in KIDlift. She rarely had time to help Ian conduct tours. Except for shoveling snow, the great team was broken up, but Ian was kept so busy with guiding school classes that he hardly had time to miss their fine-tuned exchange. John David and the other docents were scheduled with the senior bus groups and the other adult clubs and fraternal organizations that wanted to tour the exhibit. Ian was mostly on his own with the little kids.

Once he took a group of five nursery school toddlers through the exhibit. The teacher excused herself with a whisper and scurried off to HollyShop ". . . for just a peek—just a sec, okay?" The children staggered around at first, looking at the kites. One of them, a fat little boy, bumped into the icon and began to cry.

Then Ian said, "Let me show you the dragons." The respectful awe from these children filled him with a fine sense of power.

He organized them in a circle beneath the King of Dragons. Some of them looked a little scared, so Ian told them, "This is a good dragon. This is the dream dragon who guards your sleep." Then he had an inspiration.

"Turn around three times right beneath him," he said, looking seriously into their faces, "and he will hear you. He will gobble your nightmares. He will keep you safe."

Slowly, solemnly, the four little girls and the boy turned around beneath the King of Dragons.

The little boy, eyes round, exclaimed, "It works!"

When their teacher hurried guiltily back, the children and Ian were lying on the floor in a row.

Ian stood. "This is the best way to see the kites," he explained.

"Really?" The teacher was now carrying a silver shopping bag with the museum logo on it. She had done more than peek at HollyShop.

"It's a good thing I wore my slacks," she said, and promptly lay down with the children, pillowing her head with the shopping bag.

Later that week, some rough kids, unkempt boys and girls, came roaring into the gallery followed by a furious teacher.

Ian said, "I think we have something here that will interest you." His seriousness quieted them all, including the teacher, and he told them about the Japanese fighter kites and the Korean fighter kites, pointed out their spare design angled for swiftness, the clean colors, the lethal tethers. He talked of war kites and survival kites, sensing the deepness of these kids' anger, their bitterness.

December day followed December day. Sometimes Ian forgot that it would all be over come January, the tidy little salary from Plaid Lady Sam, the food, the sense of being a part of something. He forgot to change the month on the note he had left with his father's coat. He hardly ever thought of his father anymore. At night, truly tired, he fell asleep in the gallery and searched among his dreams for the remembered flight on the King of Dragons.

One day, during a lull with no tours scheduled, Ian visited KIDlift. Jean found him there. There were no little ones making kites or poetry, only Ian reading a kite book.

"I miss you," she told him. "Right now, there's only one customer in HollyShop, so I stole away."

He smiled. "Yeah. We've all been busy."

"You don't miss me at all?" She made an exaggerated pout and crossed her eyes at him.

"Of course," he said. "We are a good team." Jean sighed and wandered over to the Wishing Tree. Idly she fingered the little paper kites, some elaborately colored, some with crayon scribbles, some with only the wish. *I WISH* . . .

"Oh, listen to this, Ian. The wishes:

"To get picked for Student of the Month.

"Dolphins for Christmas—I wonder if he means real ones?

"To have all world problems to be solved and for my enemy Daryl to be nicer to me before I go insain.

"It's spelled i-n-s-a-i-n. Oh, these are hilarious! It's like eating chips," she told Ian. "Eat one and you can't stop.

"For my mom to make some new friends and try to like the snow.

"Ohhh . . .

"One milyon dollars—Ian, its spelled m-i-l-y-o-n! Oh, listen to this:

"There would be world peace and good weather for years to come.

"And, oh, listen:

"I wish I will be taller.

"I wish I could stay here.

"Wow! Who would want to stay here?" she asked. Ian abruptly stopped reading.

"I wish I saw my mom and dad for Christmas thats al I want."

Ian put the book he was reading back on the shelf.

"Only helpless people put wishes on a tree," he said without looking at Jean.

Jean read:

"No people can get a divorce and to have my own pet that's a cat and not have to share with my sister."

"Yes, they are helpless. They're just kids. But maybe wishing helps them, maybe saying the wish helps. Oh, listen to this one:

"That my dog Thor would live forever."

"No," said Ian, "it doesn't help."

"Don't you have wishes?" asked Jean.

"If I want something, I try to figure out how to get it. If I can't figure out how to get it, I stop wanting it."

"Always?"

"Always," said Ian. Then he blurted out, "I'd like to buy you lunch."

"You *do* like me," said Jean. "You don't mind being seen in public with a bald girl? My mother cringes when we go out to eat." She wiggled her eyebrows at him and then wiggled her bare ears. "Tomorrow?"

But the next day turned out to be busy right up until closing time. They had only one break, and they took the pizza Sam had ordered into KIDlift. Jean's mother showed up with some papers for her to fill out from Clonlara home-based schooling.

"Clonlara is for high school kids," Jean told

him. "But it feels like I'm applying for some boring job." She made a face.

"Mom is having a fit because the tuition is $475. My dad thinks they're throwing the money away."

She is the little girl now, thought Ian. He was impatient with his friend.

"I loved school," he told her. "I miss it. I wish I were back in school right now!" He stopped himself in horror. What was he exposing? Then he remembered: He was supposedly home-schooled, too.

But Jean just asked, "Even on Christmas vacation?"

"Yes. No," stammered Ian. "No. I mean, I like working here."

Jean studied him thoughtfully. What was she thinking?

"You're very well adjusted," she said. "You have strong character."

She sighed and picked up a pink kite shape and wrote across its face. Then she rose and hung it on the Wishing Tree.

After she left, he read it.

I wish to learn something valuable in my eighteenth year.

◆═◑◑═◆

Today the doctor was wearing a gray jogging suit. He seemed full of confidence and purpose. Patient 227 lay back on the couch. He sighed, waited, drifted.

"Well," said the doctor, finally breaking the silence, "last time you seemed to be discovering yourself. How do you feel about what you're finding out?"

The last time. The last time the doctor had given him a backpack, his backpack, to look through, to prompt memory. Familiar clothing, a comb, toothbrush and toothpaste. For a long time he held a flat case, his hands remembering the smooth hardness of it. He knew what was inside—barber scissors, tipped and sharp. His hands remembered something else—the snip against a weight of hair; the red hair falling in silent tufts. A floor littered with dark red tufts. A laugh? Was there a laugh? That tickles, Dad.

A great weariness had come soothingly into him. He had been too tired to remember more.

He was still tired, exhausted, as if he were back in the prison compound, but there at least, he had shared his exhaustion. Now he felt as if he were the only exhausted person in a foreign country filled with purposeful people. He could not remember the feeling of energy. It had taken great effort to get to the doctor's office, only one floor up from room 227 by elevator. It took great effort to think, to speak. The images in his head moved in slow motion. People and objects around him were seen as if on a dim movie screen.

With forced exertion he answered the doctor. "I feel dead."

"Why, do you suppose?"

"My body doesn't seem to manufacture food into fuel," said the patient.

"Are you eating?"

Patient 227 fought to remember. "I don't know. There was some kind of . . . of shepherd's pie. Yesterday?" He remembered it on the plate in the cafeteria.

Then, quite suddenly, hunger hit him like a storm. Had the boy eaten? What had he done to the boy? Hollowness pained his stomach. Shepherd's pie. His mouth collected saliva. There had only been some milk and peanut butter. Bread? Crackers?

"He must have eaten it by now," he said to the doctor.

"Who must have eaten what?"

"How long have I been here?" asked Patient 227, struggling up from the couch. "How long?" He could feel a surge of fear warming his body. "How long?" He was shouting at the doctor now.

A look of concern—or was it panic?—crossed the doctor's face, and the survival control that had been a part of Mitchell Bayless for a long time returned.

"Sorry," he said. He sat on the couch. "I just remembered where I left my son. I need to get to a phone."

The doctor gestured to the one on his desk. "Go ahead."

Mitchell Bayless dialed a number. The woman's voice on the other end said "Hello" three times before he could clear his throat and ask, "Mildred?"

CHAPTER SEVENTEEN

The Betrayal

"You liked second grade," Jean reminded Ian. "You liked Miss Lusk, and that was public school."

Ian was sharpening pencils while Jean pinned to the wall a bright array of kites some children had made over the weekend.

It was Monday. ARTlift was closed on Mondays, like its parent museum, the Grand River Institute of Arts, across town.

Some of the staff and a few volunteers were working to organize inventory, revise scheduling, and clean up after a week of heavy visitor traffic. Supplies in KIDlift had to be replenished, questionnaires and body counts recorded. The museum kept track of how many guests ARTlift generated and what they thought of the exhibit. It was a way of measuring the success of the program.

"It helps when we request funding or write new grants for another project," Jean's mother had explained. "That helps, and the press coverage helps."

There had been a lot of press coverage. Television people came and newspaper reporters were constantly showing up. The Lady Leader, Jean's mother, was always being interviewed and having her picture taken. Ian himself had been interviewed for the morning television show *Meet Grand River*. It had mostly been about the kite exhibit, and Ian had been able to sidestep questions like "What does your mom think about your job at ARTlift?" by talking about the marvels of kites and KIDlift. The *Grand River Press* wanted to do a feature on the boy expert, but so far Ian had managed to avoid the friendly newspaper reporter.

Now it was Jean who was trying to dig into his life. They began to sort questionnaires, which left plenty of freedom to talk.

"I mean, you liked public school. Why did your mom want to do home-schooling? What's better about it?"

"There's no schedule," said Ian, feeling around in his brain for reasons. "I mean, you make a schedule to suit yourself. And you get to do real work like this."

"That's right," mused Jean. "It counts as a credit.

And so does volunteering. You have to do three hundred hours."

Ian breathed easier. "How about trips?" he asked. He would keep her talking. He would ask the questions.

"Yes! Even my trips to Russia and to Holland; they count."

"Do you have to take tests?" asked Ian. He could keep this going forever.

"No!" squealed Jean. "Isn't that great? Well, actually there are some tests you have to take if you want credits for college. But it's not like a weekly thing."

"Does your mother help with high-school stuff?"

"No," said Jean. "It's not like elementary school. You mostly choose what you want to study. You have a contact teacher you can talk to on the phone or E-mail or write to. I should graduate in March or April if I do all the work. It's pretty interesting."

She looked at Ian, then smiled.

"Did you mean what you said a while ago? Can I read to you sometimes? I mean the stuff I decide to study? That way—well, it would be like when we trained the docents—you'll learn what I'm learning because we share it?"

Ian paused, hands full of questionnaires. He

felt his face grow warm. Perhaps they were friends forever, not just until the kites came down.

The school groups stopped coming about the same time as all the Christmas cookies began to appear in the volunteer lounge next to HollyShop. Christmas vacation had begun. The volunteers brought, besides cookies, little hors d'oeuvres and punch. Everyone began to celebrate the coming of the holiday season.

Grandparents came during the day with their grandkids. Garlands of holly and evergreen branches were hung about the entrance, making the hallway smell fresh and piney. Ian ate a lot of Christmas cookies. He had time to browse in HollyShop. The store was busy all day long now that Christmas was so close. He felt he would like to get Jean a Christmas present, but should he get one for Plaid Lady, too? The prices in HollyShop were very high. No presents. How careless he was becoming, even thinking of stuff like that. He should be thinking about what he was going to do after Christmas, after New Year's. He should be thinking about finding his dad. Or not finding him.

He should be considering public school. Now he had an address that he could try to use to get back into school. His spirits lifted. He could try that. If he got into school, he could check the mail-box on Freemont Street often for school corre-spondence.

He was relieved when Plaid Lady Sam told him to prepare for a Boy Scout troop coming in on Saturday and, after that, a large Sunday school class. He had had too much time to think.

Would he help Sue ready KIDlift, Sam wanted to know. "The whole church is coming," said Plaid Lady. "There will be several tours." Would Ian take the small and middle-sized children?

Saturday was the busiest day yet. Ian found the Boy Scouts were fascinated with the Hargrave sur-vival kite and Bell's Tetrahedron kite, which had carried a man 168 feet in the air.

Then the church group arrived. It was a mostly black church. Everyone was dressed to kill. Some ladies wore hats; some had hairstyles that put the hats to shame. There were marcelled waves and dreadlocks; there were great fluffy shapes and ini-tials cleverly shaved onto scalps; there were tiers of braids and spirals. Here and there, scattered like froth on the deeper foam, were a few white faces, a few blond heads.

"Come this way. I have something I think you'll like," Ian was saying to a group of wide-eyed chil-dren. At the edge of his vision was a man with a reddish beard, hair tied behind with a thong.

"Come this way," said Ian, his heart beginning to race.

He took the hand of one little boy, and the others started to follow.

"Ian."

Ian stopped in his tracks. Turned.

Turned to look up into the face of his father.

He didn't think he made the noise he heard—a sort of *uhhh* and a gasp.

"Ian. Ian?"

He could feel his heart, and looked down at his white shirt to see if he could see it thumping through the fabric. He noticed he was still holding the hand of the little boy, and he said, "Excuse me" to the child and dropped the warm fingers.

"Ian?" This time it was a woman's voice. A voice from the telephone. His aunt Mildred, whom he could not remember—was that her? A thin woman in a long coat and tan boots stood at the edge of the group of children. She had a stern face, hair very short.

"I saw you on morning television," she said. "They gave your name, Ian. But they got the last name wrong. Foxworth, Foxwood—something like that." Her voice was disapproving.

The room tipped and seemed to slide beneath him. He stopped it with his mind. The children backed away, and he couldn't find the energy to stop them. Something was being lost, and he couldn't do anything.

"You said . . . you said . . ." stammered Ian. He looked fiercely at his father. "You said to get your own ice cream. You said walking tall would keep me safe. I did. I did. No wishing. I walked tall. I got careless; I got a white shirt. But for a good reason, Dad. And I got better. I did. I was getting better at no traces."

His aunt was looking at him with such concern that Ian knew she wasn't seeing him. But he could tell she was full of wrong opinions. He was all right. He was doing just fine. Where had the children gone?

His father dropped his head. Neither one of them was hearing him.

"Ian, oh, my boy . . ."

"No one knows. I got rid of Delbert Joe. I can go to school. We have an address—until spring . . ."

An old feeling from years ago choked him. Why was he crying? He wiped angrily at his eyes, and the wetness infuriated him more. He began to scrub his face with his hands, then beat at his cheeks, trying to punch the crying away.

"Ian. Ian." His father's arms were pulling him close, came down around him. Held Ian's arms. Clean shirt smell and the familiar warmth. No other person. His father. He punched weakly at his father, rigid and frustrated.

Things were falling apart.

"It will be all right. It will get better," his father said.

Things were falling apart.

"You're going to stay with your aunt Mildred," said his father quietly. "You can go back to school."

Things were falling apart. Things were breaking. His father was cutting him away, cutting away his wings and Jean had cut her hair and the dragon was too high up and the clocks were spinning around and nothing was right, no matter how careful he was. All the hard and happy work didn't count. Didn't work. Nothing counted. Nothing worked. Nothing would ever be right.

CHAPTER EIGHTEEN

The King of Dragons

"At first I thought they were stealing you, Ian," said Jean. "That woman in the tan boots and the bearded, Old West–looking guy with the ponytail." His father and his aunt had been ushering him toward the main entrance when, suddenly, Ian halted and said, "I have to finish my job."

He sort of wobbled as he walked back into the gallery, had a hard time staying on a straight course. Jean had run down the hall, following him, whispering to his back, "Anything wrong? Can I help?"

Ian shook his head, shook her away.

"Those people are still standing by the doors," Jean continued. "Do you want me to go get Sam or John David?"

"They are my family," said Ian. He stopped as if

struck. "They are my family," he repeated.

"I don't even recognize them. Is that your mom?"

Ian said, "I have to show the children the kites. Then I'll bring them to you in KIDlift. There are a lot of them. I'll help you with kite making and stuff." He looked back toward the worried figures of his father and his aunt Mildred, both watching him from the entrance.

"But first I'll have to explain to my family. About my job."

"I'd like to keep you company in the gallery," offered Jean, "since there's so many kids—just to help keep track."

The arrival of Ian's family didn't help Ian do his usual easy job with the tour, one that always gave him pleasure. They sat on one of the benches, a little ways apart, his thin father and his aunt, a serious woman holding her purse in the exact center of her lap. With their eyes on him, Ian had trouble concentrating, getting ready, the way he always did, to offer up the magic of kites. Some of the children, gathered in loose groups, had lost interest. Two little boys pushed each other.

Ian struggled to collect himself, aware of Jean hovering nearby. Instinctively he moved beneath the King of Dragons, looked up into the splendid fierce head. Then, everything came together just right—like an angle of incidence—control, like a bridle in his hands.

"This is my favorite kite," he said, and after that he was okay.

Plaid Lady Sam stood, reached across her desk, and shook his father's hand. Ian sensed Jean hovering in the doorway.

"You have a remarkable young man here," said Plaid Lady, and turned an inquiring glance toward his aunt Mildred.

"This is Aunt Mildred," said Ian, feeling the words like blocks of wood splitting his mouth.

"Yes, my sister, Mildred," said his father. "I'm . . . I'm relieved Ian . . . uh . . . is prospering here. He's been no bother?" His father was trying to figure out how much to ask, how much to give away.

"He's wonderful," said Plaid Lady Sam. "He's never late; sometimes even gets here before I do."

His father glanced at Ian, a secretive look.

"He'll be staying with his aunt Mildred," said his father, "for a while."

Then it's not forever, thought Ian.

From the doorway, Jean asked respectfully, "You're not taking Ian away from us, are you?"

His aunt looked hard at Jean's shaved head, where, lately, a stubble had grown.

"No," she finally said.

Then, at Plaid Lady Sam's desperate request, his aunt Mildred agreed she would drive Ian the twenty-eight miles three times a week during the Christmas holidays to help with tours of the kite show. Until school started in January.

Jean pulled him aside as they were leaving. "I just wanted to tell you, I feel I've learned something already in the eighteenth year of my life, but I don't know what it is yet. Does that make sense?"

"Yes," said Ian. "Probably you'll know it when you grow up."

"Ah, you're right," said Jean. "I have to do that yet, don't I?"

She leaned down—she didn't have to lean far—and kissed him underneath his eye. She might have been going for his lips and missed, or his forehead—he wasn't sure. Then she gave a little laugh. He could still feel the soft press of her mouth under his eye.

"We're growing up together," she said, letting him go. "Cheers for now." She backed down the hall, waving.

Outside it was already dark. Falling snow softened the brightness from the streetlights. They walked to a car. His father stopped and put his hand on Ian's shoulder. Ian's eyes were level with the middle of his beard.

"You've grown," said his dad. "I probably don't

have to tell you to mind your aunt Mildred." He looked at the ground. "I will be getting better. I'll see you every week or so." Then he looked hard into Ian's eyes. "I was wrong."

"About everything?" asked Ian.

"No," said his father. "A survival lesson is never wasted. I told you molehills were mountains—and that was wrong—but I taught you how to climb mountains. I told you windmills were dragons—and that was wrong, too, but I did give you true ways to battle dragons."

Ian wasn't sure what he meant. So he told his father something he had learned on his own. "Windmills are very like kites." And he added, "I don't know any bad dragons."

To Ian's surprise, his father smiled. "Maybe I haven't harmed you then." He coughed and cleared his throat. "I'm very proud . . ." He shook Ian's hand.

There was someone waiting for his father in a little bus, and Ian watched him climb aboard.

It kept snowing all the way to his aunt's house. They didn't talk much.

Perhaps, thought Ian, when I go back, I will show Jean the room for miniature people. It would be a good place for her to read aloud to me. It occurred to him that his backpack was still there, stowed in a corner. Then another thought struck him.

"Dad left his winter coat," said Ian to the stranger who was his aunt Mildred. "In a storage bin in the basement."

"We'll tell him when he calls," she said. Her voice, quiet and steady, was in some long-ago way familiar.

The car was small and warm. Windshield wipers whispered back and forth in a soothing rhythm. Aunt Mildred's house, deep in the country, nestled among large trees. Light from a front window haloed out over the snow.

"You will take the bus to school," she said over her shoulder as he followed, stepping in her footprints out of habit.

There was a small Christmas tree, half trimmed, in her living room. She led him upstairs.

He was shown a bed in a room that had birds on the wallpaper and only one door. There were new pajamas lying on the bed.

"They're probably short, now that I've had a look at you," apologized his aunt Mildred. "We can get another pair later."

The room was cool; one of the windows was open a sliver at the bottom.

"I believe in fresh air," his aunt said. "If that's all right."

She did not kiss him good night or anything.

"Sleep well," was all she said, and left him to himself.

It was fine with Ian. In bed, he pulled the covers up to his chin and closed his eyes. The coziness was almost fearful; warmth collected around him.

The King of Dragons was waiting in his dream. *Welcome back.* His powerful scale-armored body was hunched beside the stone, now snow covered, where Ian knew he slept. Bits of feathery down and an irregular dry space in the snow crowned the rock's smooth top. The dragon motioned to Ian and crouched lower for him to mount behind the great blue-and-yellow wings.

On this flight, high in the cold air, Ian saw a few of the wild beasts below look up. The time was real time now. From a hill, a girl with long almost-black hair waved and waved and waved and, against the distant horizon, the other dragon, scales gleaming in a winter sun, appeared to be moving toward him.